MELT

CARRIE AARONS

Do you want your **FREE** Carrie Aarons eBook?

All you have to do is **sign up for my newsletter**, and you'll immediately receive your free book!

This book is for every working mother out there.
May you be strong. May you be super. May you drink lots of alcohol.

1

JAKE

I love the Cherry Blossom Festival.

Now as a guy, saying that may make me seem kind of soft. As if I like those little pink flowers that float from the trees at every monument dotting the national lawn.

But hear me out. It's a time when DC becomes a city of celebration, when families and groups of friends and college students put on their spring clothes and come out in droves. When the whole Capitol puts on its dancing shoes and smiles and attends parties, museum exhibits and street fairs.

Droves are a good thing for me. They're a good thing for business. Thus, I love the Cherry Blossom Festival.

And okay, maybe there is a certain ambience about those little pink flowers in the trees, but you won't hear me admitting that out loud. At least not to the ladies. Although if it gets me a leg up in that arena, then maybe I should.

I ponder the thought of all of the single women milling around my truck as I open the freezer, checking on my latest batch. Merlot and Fudge, and damn it's as good as it sounds.

"Do you really serve alcoholic ice cream?" A blonde twenty-something slurs a bit as she peers into the window of the truck.

Clearly, she's already partook in the alcohol part of this festival. "We sure do. Of course we have non-alcoholic flavors as well, for the kids and those not looking to get a buzz on. What can I get you?"

There are three people lined up behind her and it's only ten o'clock. Sweet baby Jesus, I love cherry blossom time. And so does Cones & Corks, my business. My baby. My fleet of three food trucks that roam the streets of Washington, DC providing sweet treats for kids and adults.

"How is the Pistachio Pinot?" She bats her eyelashes, and though she's about a day over twenty-one, I flirt back.

Because you know, always please the customer and all. "Delicious, the perfect treat for a hot day."

I give her my Virginia boy charm, flashing the smile and the dimple I know she's staring at.

"I'll take that then." She swishes her hips, and another four people get on line.

I quickly scoop her order, ring her up and have her sign the receipt. I'm not surprised when I get the piece of paper back with a wink, and her number scrawled at the top.

Politely, when she's out of view, I throw it in the trash bin. At thirty, I'm too old for her. And I've also sworn off women after my last disaster of a relationship.

Yep, it's just me, my laptop and a box of tissues for the foreseeable future.

Cycling through the line of customers, I chat and scoop. Hand out cards, give them the maps of where they can find this truck and the other two on any given day of the week.

"I want a Sponge Bob Popsicle!" A little voice yells from down below, and I have to peer out to see who it comes from.

Standing at the bottom of the truck is a little girl, her curly brown hair in pigtails and a little red dress hanging off her small body.

Her eyelashes blink up at me, and I wave. "Well hi there, pretty girl, I don't have any SpongeBob here, but I think I have something that you might like."

I look across the lawn, the Washington Monument shooting straight up into the sky. A frantic looking young woman jogs across the grass, a large bag slipping off her shoulder.

The minute she reaches my truck, and the little girl, her voice turns scolding. "Lennon, what did I tell you about letting go of mommy's hand?"

The little girl, who must be Lennon, shrugs, looking nothing but innocent. "Ice cream man says I can have ice cream!"

"He did, did he? I guess today I couldn't be any worse at being a parent, so fine let's get you a cone." She looks at the side of my truck, her eyes scanning the description for regular and alcoholic ice cream. "Do you really make alcoholic ice cream? Because I could use about a bottle of Cabernet in mine if so."

She sighs, her shoulders falling in defeat, and looks up. Dark brown eyes, long dark curls, a beauty mark on her left cheek, a strong, sharp jaw. Her looks resemble that of a fox's, something mysterious and sharp about her. And a niggling in my chest tells me that this person is familiar.

I smile down at them from my place above in the truck. "Well, unfortunately we only serve half the bottle in our scoops."

Surprisingly, she laughs at my corny joke, a husky, deliberate sound that makes my skin vibrate. "Of course, just my luck. What do you have for this girl?"

She points to her daughter, and again I feel like I know her from somewhere. "Hold on a second ..."

Going into the truck, I make up a cone of Cookie Bar Crunch for the girl, the usual flavor I recommend for kids. And I get a cup for her mom, expertly pressing two round scoops of my favorite, Oreo Peanut Butter, into it.

"And here we are. I held off on the alcohol ... unless you

weren't kidding, I could just hand over the bottle of Merlot I made my last batch with." Part of me hoped that she loved the flavor as much as I did.

Lennon tore right into the cone, getting drops of it on her red dress and not caring in the least. Kids were amazing like that. Her mom took a tiny spoonful and carefully put it in her mouth, her lids fluttering when the taste hit her tongue. And shit, I think I had a semi right then.

"That is incredible, oh my God. Wow. Okay, kid, you did good finding this ice cream man. How much do I owe you?" She looks up at me.

"It's on the house. Cute kid discount." I was shamelessly flirting by giving her free ice cream, but hey, I was the boss and I did what I wanted.

"Stop it, really, that's too much. Let me pay. This is quality stuff." She shuffles her feet, that big bag weighing down her shoulder.

"I should know, I make it. But no, it's on the house." I hesitate, still feeling a connection to her. "Hey, this may be weird, but do I know you from somewhere?"

She studies me closer, those big brown eyes inspecting my face. "I'm not sure ... did you grow up around here?"

"I've been around here for a while. Since college actually."

She tilts her head to the side, her curls blowing in the wind. "I went to Madison College, maybe that's where I know you from?"

Suddenly it all clicks. Her face a little younger, that perky butt in gym shorts. "You were a freshman when I was a senior! I worked in the gym, goofy kid in the red polo at the front. Jake Brady." I sound so desperate, trying to get her to remember me. But I used to have a major crush on this girl.

"Hmm ... I kind of remember. Sorry! Most days my brain is the consistency of scrambled eggs living with this little one." She points to Lennon. "I'm Samantha, I'm not sure if we ever officially met."

Not really, since I was too chickenshit to go after the innocent freshman back then. Lennon, now done with her ice cream, starts pulling on Samantha's jeans. "Mommy, we go see Dorothy now?"

Samantha chuckles but ruffles her daughter's hair. "Yes, we can go see her *shoes*. Dorothy herself isn't there, though." Turning up to me, she rolls her eyes. "What three-year-old is obsessed with the *Wizard of Oz*? I used to be petrified of those flying monkeys, but not her. Thanks for the ice cream, and nice to see you again!"

She waves as Lennon pulls on her, dragging her toward the Smithsonian Museum of American History.

I watch as they amble to the line, a ball of energy and fun chaos surrounding them. Samantha. I couldn't remember her last name, maybe I never knew it.

But for the rest of the day, as I served and promoted, my thoughts kept straying to the sexy freshman who had just tumbled back into town.

Alone time. Sweet, sweet alone time. Finally.

As any mom, especially single mom, knows ... the times in your bed to do whatever you want are few and far between.

"Ashley" by Big Sean bumps quietly out of my laptop speakers as I surf my Facebook timeline. I get distracted and click on some celebrity drama bait, falling into the black hole that is the Internet.

After about twenty minutes, I blink, shaking my head and leaning it back against the headboard. This week has been a whirlwind, and that's putting it lightly. Coordinating movers, setting Lennon up with daycare for the days my mom can't watch her, getting ready for my new position, trying to show my daughter the city that I once called home.

And now call home again. It's her new home too, and I've been trying to make it as fun of an experience as possible. Taking her to the monuments, teaching her the history she can understand, showing her things like Dorothy's slippers at the Smithsonian.

So far, she's been great. Well, as great as a three-year-old who bores easily and wants a snack every five seconds can be. She only asked about Derek once, and after explaining that her daddy was still in Seattle, she dropped it. I hate to sound like the bitter, scorned woman ... but it's not like he spent much time trying to make himself a part of her life. I should have seen it the day she was born, his indifference, his need for exploration not squashed. Lennon had become my biggest adventure, and the man who had helped create her wanted to travel the world without consequences.

Blowing out a breath, I can't help the sour taste that settles in my mouth. I'm being melodramatic. I chose to leave, to come home and set up a life for my daughter. No looking back now, even if my heart was broken.

But you know what fixes broken hearts? Wine and a little bit of ice cream. Picking up the stemless glass from my bedside table, I take a sip of the Riesling I'd had chilling in the fridge since we moved into our two bedroom apartment in Crystal City. It was the perfect place, with tall windows and a community pool downstairs. And without a man, I was allowed to decorate in whatever style I wanted.

The wine bubbled as it slid down my throat, and my thoughts flitted to the ice cream truck from today's list of activities. The cute guy who was working behind the window. What was his name?

Jake. I think.

A blush of embarrassment heats my cheeks. I hadn't recognized him, and even though he'd explained our connection, I still couldn't place him. It was one of those awkward scenarios where you knew that the other person knew more about you than you knew about them ... and you felt bad about it.

But he *was* cute.

Not that dating was something on a twenty-seven-year-old single mom's to-do list. Please, most mornings I was lucky if I got out of the house with my hair brushed and a shirt not stained with Lennon's cereal. But single moms could have fantasies, and maybe cute ice cream guy would be mine.

Resigning myself to the fact that I should get all the sleep I could afford, I switched off the light and settled into bed. Sleeping alone was a new phenomenon for me, something I hadn't done in nearly eight years.

And I wasn't about to lie and say I hated it. Sleeping alone was kind of excellent. So I stretched myself out all over the queen bed, and fell into a peaceful night's rest.

"**M**OMMY!"

I growled, literally grated my teeth together, while the water ran over my body. I'd only gotten in here two seconds ago after putting Lennon in front of the TV with her Lucky Charms. Sugar and entertainment were a no-no in all of the parenting magazines, but what the hell did they know? They weren't trying to get a rambunctious three-year-old out the door on time on their first day in a new job.

"I'll be right there!" I shouted, praying she'd let me get conditioner in my hair before stumbling into my morning shower session.

"Mommy, I want to wear my Winnie the Pooh costume to Mimi's today." Too late, little lady was officially in the bathroom, sitting on the closed toilet with her baby blanket grasped firmly in her fist.

Doing the quickest wash of my body possibly in history, I turned the shower off and grabbed my towel. "You can't wear a Halloween costume, sweetheart, it's April."

"But Mimi likes it, so I can wear it." Oh, the logic of a toddler.

"How about we find some clothes for you, and you can bring

your stuffed Tigger for the day instead." Distraction and compromise; two of the best tools in a mother's arsenal.

I hurry into my room, Lennon hot on my heels, as I put my hair in a towel and begin to dress in the clothes I laid out last night.

"Can you please go into your room and put on the outfit Mommy laid out?" I put a tinge of sweetness in my tone, hoping she will obey.

"I want fruit snacks." Dear God, of course you do.

She toddles out of my room, going to do lord knows what, but I need to finish myself before I can start on her. Blow drying my hair so that at least it's not sopping wet, I swipe on some mascara and lipstick and consider it a job decently done.

"Lennon Rose, you better be in your room getting dressed." Mommy voice in full effect.

When I walk in, she's in nothing but her underwear, laying on the bed talking to a stuffed owl.

"Into your clothes, please." I pick up the summer shorts and shirt I'd laid out, and shove them over her little body. At least she complies, then letting me slide her feet into sandals and allowing me to buckle them.

"Mommy, did I used to drink your milk?" Lennon looks at my boobs, the opening to my sleeveless sweater down by her tiny face.

"You did, once upon a time." A simpler time, a time where you didn't ask questions like that. Especially not in public.

"Can I drink from my own?" She looks down at her chest.

I bite back a laugh, internally panicking as I look at the clock. "No you cannot. Now let's go, get your bag and stuffed Tigger."

With one bite of toast in my stomach, I shepherd us out the door and down to the garage, loading my daughter into the car and starting to drive for my mother's house.

One *huge* plus of coming back to Washington, DC was that my mom lived ten minutes from us. She could watch Lennon during the day, save me a ton of money, and was a familial lifeline exactly at the time I needed her.

The morning was a tornado of hustling, tears, kisses, traffic and paperwork. When I finally sat down to my desk, files and files stacked upon it, I took a deep breath.

"Knock, knock." Someone proceeded the action with speech.

Turning my head, a woman stood in the doorway to my small office. "Oh, hi. Sorry, I feel like it's the first time I've sat down all day."

"And it's only nine o'clock, so you better take a few minutes." She smiles conspiratorially. "I'm Jenna, I work in the office next door, so I thought I'd come over and introduce myself. You know, in case you need to borrow a paper clip or something."

Her expression is open and friendly, her blue eyes and short blond bob pretty but smart, and I like her immediately. I extend a hand and she takes it. "Samantha Groff. I'll stop over if I need a stapler, but don't worry, I won't steal it."

She laughs. "You're the new manager of the park rangers, right?"

I nod. "Yep, I am." My phone rings, the first call of the day. "And that is probably a ranger right now."

"Take it, I'll stop over before lunch to see if you need anything. Good luck, and welcome!"

I take the call, suddenly flung into a crisis in Utah where two of the Jeeps have gone missing. Just another day in the life of a National Parks employee, but damn do I love my job. After college, I wasn't sure what I wanted to do. I followed Derek out to Seattle, and just happened to fall into a job at Mount Rainier. For five years I worked my way up, pausing for a bit in the middle when I got pregnant with the huge surprise that is Lennon. And then my dream job came along back home, and I jumped at it. Used all of my connections within the organization, interviewed through rounds and directors, and finally landed the position.

It cost me the guy in the whole dream life scenario, but looking back, I wouldn't change a thing.

Around one, Jenna pops her head in again. "Want to grab a bite? You look like you could use it, plus these walls are thin, and your phone has been ringing off the hook."

"Does that lunch come with a margarita? Because I could really use one." I survey the stacks of papers I've tried to organize on my desk.

"If you won't tell, I won't." She winks, her cute floral midi dress swaying as I follow her out.

At least I get lunch with an adult for once. There aren't sippy cups or sing-alongs in sight.

3

"Lennon, don't put that paintbrush on the carpet ..."

I walk into my mom's house a little afraid to see what's actually happening. "Hello?"

"Mommy!" I hear a shriek from the living room, and a smocked Lennon comes running at me.

I manage to pick her up before she hugs around my new black work skirt with paint all over her, and smack a kiss on her cheek. "How's my girl?"

"We're painting fingers!"

"I believe we are finger painting, but it's whatever you choose, my dear." My mom comes up behind her, and I smile a thank you at her. "Now go clean up so we can eat dinner."

"Oh, Mom, you didn't have to do that." I follow her into the kitchen, the smell of meatloaf coming from the oven.

"Hush, I didn't want you to have to cook after your first day. Tell me, how was it?"

I fill her in on the events of the day as we set the small island together, pulling out the stools and setting up Lennon's booster chair on one. She pours water and wine for the two of us, and it makes me smile that she knows I need a little red to take the edge off today.

"Did you meet anyone nice? Make a friend?" My mom still talked to me sometimes like I'd just gotten off the bus from middle school.

"Everyone is nice so far, but you know ... they all had their day one faces on. Give it a week." I shrug, not kidding myself that people are on their best behavior when they first meet you.

Mom takes the food from the counter, setting serving dishes full of delicious looking items on the island.

"Lennon, go wash your hands, dinner is ready."

"Okay, Mimi!" Her tiny feet patter on the floor as she runs for the powder room in my mom's home.

It was strange being back in my childhood kitchen, the one my family had dined in thousands of times. To see the pictures of my brother, Charlie, as a kid holding a baseball. Now he was in Africa, leaving behind our mom as well to go save lives in the jungle. The especially painful pictures were those of my father, smiling and holding us as if he'd never let us go. A heart attack had taken him when I was just fifteen, and the memory of it still haunted some of this house.

Tinkling music notes snap me out of my reverie, and I look towards the front door. "What is that?"

"Ice cream truck!" Lennon bolts from the bathroom, running to press her nose up against the glass of the screen door.

My mom wipes her hands on a dish towel and goes for her purse. "You may have one scoop before dinner, no more. And only because it's summer and Mimi can't get enough of that Lemon Poppy Seed flavor that man sells."

They both walk out, my mom grabbing my daughter's hand as they make their way to the curb. I follow, curious and also annoyed that my daughter is going to have sweets before dinner.

Walking out the front door into my mom's Alexandria cul-de-sac, I'm surprised when the same truck that Lennon ran up to two days ago pulls around the circle of pavement.

Cones & Corks is emblazoned on the side of the bright teal truck, with a picture of a delicious looking triple scoop next to a glass of wine sitting next to the words. A couple of other families in the neighborhood run to catch the truck, children yelling and waving a precious dollar in their hands. A few of them get to the truck before Lennon as it stops on a certain part of the sidewalk, and I increase my pace to make sure my daughter has only one scoop.

As I join my mom and Lennon in line, I can't help but stretch my neck to see who is inside the truck. The sun glints in my eyes and I can't make out the body attached to the hand serving melting scoops.

But by the time we get to the front of the line, I see that it's Jake. The cute guy who gave us free ice cream and knew my name. The one who looked at me with those sparkling green eyes and for a second I forgot where I was.

"Hi!" Lennon looks up at him, and I can't help but smile.

My daughter may have grown up in a home that was laced with tension, but it doesn't seem to have affected her. In fact, I often have to stop her from hugging strangers, or mannequins at the mall.

"Well hi again ... Lennon, right? I think you liked our cookie flavor last time." He directs that charming grin on her, and she nods her head emphatically.

"How does Jake know our little girl?" My mom turns to me.

"Hey, Molly!" Jake waves at my mom, and I swear she blushes like a schoolgirl.

"Why does the ice cream guy know *your* name?" I raise my eyebrow at her.

She goes up to order her Lemon Poppy Seed, and his eyes

find me at last. "Do you live in the neighborhood?" As if catching himself, he laughs. "Wow, that wasn't creepy at all."

I have to laugh, because it was kind of forward. Mom ushers Lennon back into the driveway, both of them licking at their sweet treats. "Said the grown man riding around in an ice cream truck."

His smile drops, and I instantly feel bad. "I didn't mean ..."

"No, it's okay." He chuckles. "I typically don't do the night routes, or any of the neighborhoods. I employ some college kids to do the big legwork, but one called out sick today and so it's this thirty-year-old hanging out the window tonight."

He employed them? "So the trucks are yours?"

"They better be, with as much money as I pay for the permits and maintenance. What can I get you tonight, Samantha?"

Something about the way he said my name, and the fact that he owned his own business, made my stomach flutter. Oh, the things that turned me on these days ... I couldn't decide whether I was more impressed by his dimple or his job status.

"Oh, I'm okay, we were just about to have dinner. Can't spoil my appetite."

Jake leans out of the truck window, his bicep flexing out of his light green T-shirt. "Life is short, eat dessert first."

I'm so sex-starved these days that I instantly imagine him pushing me up against a freezer in his truck. Shaking my head, because oh my God how embarrassing that I'm having my fantasy right in front of the real life man, I try not to stutter when I open my mouth.

"Okay, what do you recommend?"

He holds up a finger, as in "give me a minute" and disappears into the truck. He comes back with a single scoop in a cup, the ice cream a mint green.

"I just thought this up this morning. Mint chocolate chips

with peppermint schnapps mixed in. The chocolate chunks are from this local DC chocolatier I work with, try it."

He seems so excited about the flavor that I kind of get excited too. Taking the spoon, I ladle a small amount into my mouth. And proceed to die from food orgasm.

"Oh my God, that is heaven." I think I may close my eyes. And my knees may go weak.

The smile on his face is cocky when I open my eyes. "I'm pretty good at what I do, and that's just a fact. So how do you know Molly?"

The sun is setting over the back of the truck, and he probably has a route to get back to but it doesn't seem like he's leaving anytime soon. And even though Mom and Lennon have gone inside, I don't have the urge to join them just yet. Maybe it's the fact that I haven't gotten real male attention in a long time, but this is nice. Even if Jake isn't flirting with me, but *come on* I totally think he is, it's nice to just banter with a man.

"She's actually uh ... my mom."

His face goes full of surprise. "No way?! What a small world. I started on this route when I was just starting out, and she has been a loyal customer for three years."

I nod, not knowing what else to say now. "Well ... I should probably head inside and eat dinner. It was uh ... good to see you again."

Raising my hand in a wave, I start to walk back up the sidewalk, cursing myself for being awkward and so off my game from years of not speaking to other men.

"Hey, Samantha?" His voice floats over my ears. I turn, waiting for him to speak. "I know that you don't really remember me, but we've now bumped into each other twice ... and I'd be stupid not to ask. Would you want to get dinner with me sometime?"

Now I really do blush, unused to being asked out on a date.

Especially by someone who seems to go after whatever he wants, all honesty.

Inside, my heart strings tug. So many things circle in my head. Lennon. Derek. My age. My life right now. Wanting to live a little. Deciding I am still young. Needing something outside of my everyday routine.

"Sure, I'd like that." I nod, as if making up my own mind in that moment and promising to myself.

For the first time in eight years, I give a man my phone number. And try not to scream like a teenage girl while I walk back inside, thinking about when he might call and what I might wear.

4

The machines whir as I walk by them, inspecting them like soldiers in a row. Gleaming massive, silver canisters, my pride and joy, churning my latest brain children.

"How you doing today, Betty?" I lay a hand on the second machine, rubbing it like a genie's lamp.

"You know they can't actually hear you, right?" The snarky voice comes from the doorway.

Leaning against it is Alice, my business partner slash sommelier slash therapist slash savior. When I decided to forge out on my own and start a business, much to the dismay of my family, I'd bumped into the tattooed, tough-talking woman in front of me, and we'd hit it off. She'd haunted the DC foodie scene for years, working in bars and eateries. She knew her shit, knew the ins and outs of what tasted good, what marketing sold, what we needed to do to get our business out to the masses. With my business degree, good-boy attitude and determination, we made quite a team.

I take in her hair, a shade of deep purple this week, and smirk. "It's the secret to our success, so don't knock it."

"And here I was, thinking I was the special sauce to this business. Hey, the new pinots are in from California, and they're fucking delicious." She cracks her knuckles, her nose piercing glinting as she walks into what we call "the kitchen."

Our office is a small building on the outskirts of the city, nice enough that it doesn't get broken in to, but cheap enough that it takes me forty-five minutes to get out here in traffic. The perimeter is fenced under a key code so we can keep the trucks here overnight, and all of our operations are handled under one roof.

"Taste test tonight, then? Tell Jana and we'll set up the conference room."

Taste test was code word for "let's drink all of the new stock to quote unquote, see how it would fit into recipes we'd been dreaming up." It was key for business, but it also gave us an excuse to kick back a little as an office. Along with Alice, we had a part time receptionist and bookkeeper, Jana, and two college students turned drivers who were with us most of the year, Ben and Freddie. Other than the five of us, we had rotating temp drivers that I'd come to trust and worked with a time or two if we were in a jam.

"Got it, how did the drive go? Sorry you had to drive the truck, Manny just couldn't fill in today." Alice walks into the hall and I follow, bypassing the three office doors until I reach the large conference room at the end of the building.

"Eh, it's no big deal. Plus, I got a girl's number." I give her a charming smile; the one I know she'll roll her eyes at.

She smiles that shit-eating grin, the one that makes me nervous. "I got a girl's number too, and I bet mine's hotter than yours."

As well as being a kickass business partner, Alice is also a player. She's one of the only people, man or woman, I know that has a rotating schedule of sexy, single women climbing in and out of her bed. I'd almost admire her if she hadn't stolen girls right out from under my nose numerous times.

"I don't think so, this one … she's gorgeous." I think of Samantha's face, the mystery lurking beneath the mommy facade.

"Don't you remember what happened the last time you got a girl's number in the truck?" She raises a dark eyebrow at me.

I cringe at the blond who'd keyed one of the trucks after I did her in it and never called her again. My conscience shudders and guilt roils in my gut. "Well, this one is a little different."

"Are you blushing, dude? Wowwwww. Who is she?" Alice pushes my shoulder.

I set up the conference table for a tasting, with the mini-wine glasses, spit buckets, plates for fudge and cheese. "She's a woman, a grown-ass woman. And that's all you need to know for now."

Alice stops, like a frozen caricature of herself. "Who are you and what have you done with Jake Brady? Damn, I think I need to meet her."

I laugh, brushing her off. But in all honesty, since I saw Samantha this afternoon in that cul-de-sac, all I've been thinking about is using the number that she gave me. And typically, I'm not the type to chase a girl. Sure, I've picked up my fair share, more than, and we have a fling and it's sexy and fun … but that's usually it. If any of them had ever introduced me to their kid, I'd have hightailed it the other way. If a woman snubbed me years ago, only to not act too interested, or not even know my name, when I saw her again … I would have turned and hooked the closest ten with a mini-skirt on. And that sounds shallow, but I've never felt like pursuing anyone.

Until now, I guess. I hadn't gone after her at college all those years ago, and I was not dumb enough to ignore fate knocking on my door. That sounded so cliché, but then again, I'd admitted that I liked flowering trees not too long ago so I was surprising myself in all kinds of ways these day.

"Let's get to it." Jana came in rubbing her hands together. "I've got two hours before I have to go home and play wife and mom, and I plan to do that with at least a great buzz, so show me the money."

Her husband was an ear, nose and throat doctor who worked long hours, and she had two little boys at home who were cute, but a handful. I'd only babysat them once, but after I'd slept for about three days I was so exhausted.

"Are we waiting for the drivers?" I asked, not knowing whether to put out more supplies.

"Screw that." Alice grabbed the farm fresh cheese and home-made fudge from the fridge. "Those newbs don't even know a Pinot from a pineapple. More wine for us, and plus, I don't need to fraternize with children today."

Jana laughs and takes a seat, pouring herself a proper tasting size out of one the bottles lined up on the table. Alice and I sat down on the other side of the table, taking glasses and pouring for ourselves. We sip in silence for awhile, the sun setting outside the windows.

"Yuck ..." Alice spits into one of the stainless steel containers. "Tastes like moldy vagina."

Jana lets out a sharp laugh and her cheeks go pink, our kind of humor a little crude for her still.

"That's the worst kind of vagina." I shake my head in mock dismay.

"No, the worst kind is no kind, and you my friend are in a dry spell. I know it, just by the look in your eyes." Alice takes a sip of a new wine, and writes down something about the notes.

While she's a vulgar jokester, her mind for alcohol and marketing is whip sharp, and I'm a lucky guy for her to have found me when this idea sparked in my head.

And she's also a mind reader, because I haven't told her about my lack of dates or female company lately. "What are you, the relationship whisperer?"

Jana, a little tipsy and not as experienced in holding her liquor, giggles. "It's like she can look into your soul and tell that you haven't gotten laid in a while. Quick Alice, tell me if my husband is going to give me a real Fifty Shades experience!"

"It is decidedly so." Her purple locks shake as she nods her head and moves on to the next bottle.

"The magic eight ball of pussy and dick, everyone." I sigh, leaning back in my chair.

"Just let me know if you'd like me to work my magic. I don't like to see any genital go hungry." She bows her head like she needs to pray for me.

This was the perfect way to end the night, with my feet up drinking good wine and working on my business. The only thing that would make it better is using the number that was burning a hole in my pocket.

But I was going to bide my time, and I needed a clear head when I finally reached out to Samantha.

So for now, I would let my imagination wander into creation land, thinking up flavors and new possibilities.

5

SAMANTHA

The phone rings just as I'm about to get up from my desk, and I sigh, my shoulders sore and my brain frazzled.

"Samantha Groff, National Parks, how can I help you?" I set my overflowing purse, which more resembles an entire country, on the floor next to me.

It's been a trying, but rewarding, Friday, and all I want to do is get out of here.

"Hi, Samantha, it's Elvin. I just wanted to say thank you for helping with the situation before. I know we were probably clipped with you, but I just wanted to let you know how crucial your help was at the time."

Internally I melt, sometimes needing to hear how good I am at my job. Because I know it, I'm damn good. But in the heat of the moment during the day, with all of the crisis that falls across my desk, I'm rarely thanked. To them, I'm just management, sitting in some corporate office dictating policy and procedure. But some of them know that I've been in the field, that I could handle these tasks with my bare hands if I were left to it.

"Well, that's very nice of you, Elvin, and I'm just doing my job. Just ... next time you have a bunch of wild animals break loose, teach your rangers the proper technique to tangle them back up." I laugh, signaling my joke.

But really, I don't know why it got that out of hand that they had to call me in. *Men*, I swear.

"Will do, you have a great weekend now."

I wish him the same and hang up, practically sprinting from the office before I can get pulled back into one more conversation. In the parking lot, Jenna waves as she gets into her Honda truck, and I wave back at my new friend. Over the past week or so, we've eaten together every day, and she's given me some tips about life in the national office. There is more red tape, also known as bullshit, to deal with. People who I should avoid, and those who I should press my lips against their ass. She's been a good ally, and has rather funny anecdotes to get me through the day sometimes.

I'm just about to start the engine to my little red Camry when my phone pings with a text message. Before Lennon, which I refer to as BL because my life changed so much after becoming a parent, I would have checked it while driving. But I'm trying to set a good example, blah blah, and so I put the keys down and pick up the phone before venturing out onto the road.

Derek: *Thinking about coming out to see you both. Missing the girly. Would that be okay?*

I sigh and rest my head back against the seat. You've got to be kidding me. Almost a month has gone by since we left Seattle, and I've barely heard from him. And now, *now* that we're finally getting settled, he wants to jostle Lennon with a visit when I know he won't stay.

I told him when I left, our argument awkward and not heated like it should have been for a woman and man who were splitting up after eight years, that I would never keep him from his daughter. And I meant it.

But I also knew Derek, and I knew that this idea was probably spur of the moment, and would pass within the hour.

Samantha: *Sure, that would be fine. She would love to see you. Just let me know your plans and/or dates.*

Jesus, help me. I hadn't seen my bearded, mountain man of an ex in almost a month, and surprisingly, I hadn't been hurting all that much. Our relationship had gone downhill after Lennon was born. And by downhill, I meant that Derek just seemed to vanish. It was like his inability to be a good father completely turned me off to him as a boyfriend.

Sure enough, three minutes later and still no response. Not even any little bubbles indicating that he was typing, or thinking of a plan. I knew right then that he wasn't serious about flying across the country to see his daughter. And while that was sad, I was also kind of selfishly happy.

Buckling my seatbelt and heading for the highway home, I was surprised when my cell began to ring through the Bluetooth. With the delay of the car, stupid technology, I wasn't able to read the name who was calling on the dashboard, and I just picked it up thinking it was either my mom. Or less likely, Derek, wanting to talk about a visit.

"Hello?"

"Hi, Samantha, it's Jake. How was your week?"

Instantly my heart drops and beads of sweat gather at the back of my neck, and I feel like I should pull over to the side of the road because no way can I have this conversation while driving.

But I'm in bumper to bumper and there is no way I can leave the babysitter with Lennon any longer. My daughter might have eaten her whole as it is.

"Ja ... Jake, nice to hear from you." Was it? Since I'd given him my number, I'd thought about him calling until I was shaking my legs in bed like a fifteen-year-old girl. "My week was

... well it was hectic to be honest, but I'm happy it's Friday. How was yours?"

It felt strange having this conversation with a man, a very sexy man, while a pair of my daughter's underpants sat on the passenger seat along with a half empty canister of animal crackers and a stack full of grocery store coupons. If that didn't depict my life right there, nothing did.

"It was pretty good, but I wanted to make it even better. Would you go out with me tomorrow night?"

"Damn, you cut right to the chase, don't you?"

I slap a hand over my mouth, completely appalled that I just said that out loud.

A husky laugh comes through my Bluetooth. "In fact I do, but normally people like that quality in a man."

He was kind of right. "I am so sorry, now I've shown just how rusty I am at this whole conversation, not to mention dating, thing."

"So that's a yes, then? You'll go on a date with me?" I can practically see his smug, charming smile at the other end of the phone.

Thumbing through the mom-calendar in my head, I determined that I had nothing planned for Saturday night. And why not go? I mean, he wasn't a total stranger, which eliminated the awkward "Is he a serial killer?" debate that one sometimes had when trying to date again. And he was cute. Had a job. Seemed relatively down-to-earth. If my correspondence with Derek was any clue, I no longer had feelings for my ex. Who said a single mother couldn't also find love?

Well, almost every ounce of time on the clock and a petulant three-year-old, but that was beside the point.

"If I can get a sitter, sure I will." I slipped in the part about Lennon because I wanted this guy to know now, my daughter came first.

"Why don't you bring her along? We can do something PG." The way he said it implied that he wanted to do non-PG things with me, and it made my thighs tingle.

But my heart also fluttered, in a way it hadn't in a long time. Not that I'd had much experience other than Derek, but the fact that a man, who wasn't my daughter's father, wanted to include her in a date ... well, the significance wasn't lost on me.

"That would be ... really nice, thanks. Should I give you some ideas or—"

"No need, I have some up my sleeve." His voice was mysterious and boyish, and suddenly, I didn't know who would enjoy this date more, Lennon or me.

"All right, just nothing with slime or Jell-O, I'm not trying to clean up a mess."

"You're telling this to a guy who makes ice cream for a living. I practically live mess. But okay, I'll abide by your rules. I'll pick you two up, now that you have my number, text me your address."

Alarm bells went off. A stranger having my address, Lennon's car seat in someone else's car, was he even a good driver? Mentally, I slapped myself. I had to stop this. I'd promised myself when I moved here that the mania and worrying would lessen. That I'd give life a chance to surprise me more, and take me where I was supposed to go.

"Sounds like a date." I try to use my flirtiest tone possible, and I think I kind of achieve it.

We hang up, my heart still doing that two step it had picked up ever since Jake's voice came through the car stereo.

And then I went into full on panic mode again. Because Jesus, what the hell was I going to wear?

Smoothing down the maroon colored blouse I'd decided on, my eyes shifted to the window again. I was already nervous enough about my first date in eight years, but the fact that another man would be driving my child around was what was making my heart really pound.

Mentally cataloging, I made sure I had everything I'd need in this stripped-down diaper bag. Lennon's car seat was on the floor next to us, ready to be put in Jake's car as soon as he showed up. He'd insisted on driving, something I was having a hard time letting go of control for.

I was showing up to this date with literal baggage. I let out a quick laugh, thinking that if he could handle that, then the man must be too good to be true.

"Mommy, where we go?" Lennon danced around the lobby of our apartment building, jigging to some imaginary music in her head.

"We're going on a little adventure with a friend." I stared out the glass front doors again.

"Yeah, but where?" Her questions never stopped these days.

"You'll see when we get there." I couldn't very well tell her that I wasn't sure myself, because this would only attract more attention and questions.

My palms were sweaty, and I examined my white jeans and simple white Keds. I'd gone cute and casual for the date, but was a little daring with my white before Memorial Day. My long dark hair was down, blown dry thanks to a few minutes of Sesame Street distracting Lennon. And I was panicking. At least I had a buffer in my daughter, and an excuse if the "date" got weird or I just wasn't feeling it.

Part of the reason I was a little schitzy was because before now, I guess I hadn't allowed myself to really appreciate how attractive Jake was. Sure, I'd had a few fleeting images of him since we'd met, or I guess seen each other again, outside of the monuments. He had that classic movie star look, like James Dean or Guy Madison. Pure American male, the brown hair dusted with gold, and a dimple to boot. I hadn't seen him standing outside of his truck yet, but from what I'd seen, I wasn't going to be disappointed.

"Park! I want to go see ducks!" Lennon grabbed onto my leg, pulling at my shirt.

Back in Seattle, I would take her to the park almost every Saturday to throw little bread crumbs at the ducks in the pond. It was the first time she'd asked me since we'd moved, and I guess I now had to find a similar park somewhere close to us.

"Hey." A male voice and the glinting of the sun off glass as the lobby doors open attracted my attention.

Damnnnnn. Would it be inappropriate for me to whistle?

Jake strolled across the lobby on long, jean clad legs, his body large and lean, taking up space even though the ceilings were vaulted. His hair was brushed back but still a little wild, his muscular arms peeking out of a dark gray T-shirt that showcased the sculpted body underneath. A grin covered his full lips, the dimple popping out and making my stomach drop.

This man looked like one of those supermodels for Abercrombie & Fitch, but all grown up. Like at any moment, you could pop him on a beach on Nantucket with a classic pigskin football in his hands and he would look totally natural. If Derek was anything to go by, Jake was completely opposite of my type. I liked beards and tattoos, a little rough around the edges. It was odd that this man, who I embarrassingly did not remember from college, was doing something for me.

"Hi, Jake." I smiled back, genuinely happy to be doing something different this Saturday.

"Ice cream!" Lennon ran to him, holding out her hands like he was going to provide her with a loaded cone from his back pocket.

He chuckled, bending down to her level. "Hey, Lennon, good to see you. I don't have any ice cream today, but maybe we'll get you something later." He looked up at me, green eyes taking in my entire body. "If it's okay with your mom, of course."

My daughter doesn't even look at me. "It's okay, promise."

I roll my eyes as he stands. "You can see who the boss is around here."

"I'll be sure to remember that. It's good to see you, you look really nice." He leaned in, his lips meeting my cheek for the briefest of seconds, sending tingles across my skin.

The move was a statement; while my daughter might be accompanying us, this was definitely a date. My heart rate kicked up.

A tiny hand reached out from below and latched onto Jake's. Looking down, Lennon had already claimed his as her own.

"We go now?" She looked up at him with her big brown eyes, and I swear I saw the minute he fell under her spell.

I hiked the bag on my shoulder up and bent to retrieve her car seat, but it was lifted before I could pull it up.

"I got it. Need me to take that too?" He held the car seat like it weighed nothing, while Lennon gripped his other hand.

Jeez. My ovaries may have swooned. "I've got it. So where *are* we going?"

We walk to his car, a smaller black SUV, and he fishes out his keys to unlock it.

"Who's more impatient, you or your daughter?" He smirks, his dimple mesmerizing me.

He was teasing me, and I liked it. It felt better that he wasn't trying to yes me to death, or act like an overly-smooth gentleman. I smiled to myself as I put Lennon's car seat in the back, strapping it in well.

"I sit up front." Lennon crossed her little arms across her chest and gave that pouty lip that made me want to scream and kiss her at the same time.

"Maybe in a year or two, big girl. But for now, why don't you help me navigate from the back seat? I need someone to help me look out the windows."

Jake seamlessly pacified her, and she climbed up and into her seat with his help. Amazed, I silently buckled myself into the passenger seat, noting how clean his car was.

"Did you get your car cleaned for today?" I had my suspicions, and it just popped out.

As he slid his seatbelt across his broad torso, he paused. "Is it that obvious?"

I titled my head and smiled. "It smells like that nice wash the professional carwash uses, and there are no crumbs in your cup holders. I should probably never have you in my car."

Jake kept his eyes on the road, but I could feel the proximity now of my body to his. Lennon hummed in the back, occupying herself like she sometimes did.

"So how was your week?" He breaks the silence.

I sigh, resting into the seat because I'm glad it's the weekend. "Busy, but productive. I'm getting up and running at work, trying to settle us both. It's been an adjustment, but it's nice to be home."

I couldn't remember what he studied at Madison, and I hoped he didn't know more about me than I knew about him going into this. Honestly, I couldn't even remember him from back then, which showed how much attention I must have been paying to overlook a guy like Jake.

"And what is it that you do? Sorry, I can't remember what you were studying. Not that I knew or anything ... we barely said hi in college. I wasn't some creep."

That made me laugh, because maybe we were thinking the same things. "Good to know. I work for the National Parks Departments as a ... coordinator of sorts. I'm the contact in the national office for every park ranger around the country."

Jake weaves us through traffic as he raises an eyebrow. "Impressive. Is that what you went to school for?"

It was nice to have someone genuinely asking about what I did. It wasn't often that I got to talk about my career, something that I was, in fact, very proud of.

"Actually no, not at all. I went to become a teacher and kind of ... ended up working for a national park out in Seattle after school." I didn't know if I should disclose anything about Derek, or the relationship I'd had with Lennon's father.

Was that too heavy for a first date? Then again, I had brought my three-year-old so, clearly, he knew I wasn't a snow white virgin.

"That's cool, and now you're big time, huh? I bet you're awesome." He smiled, casting a quick glance on me. "I didn't know you grew up in the area."

We take a turn off the highway onto familiar territory, and I try to guess in my head where he might be taking us. "Yep, went to high school just outside near my mom's house in Virginia. How about you, was Madison close to home?"

Jake's hands grip the steering wheel, his big fingers flexing and controlling the car with ease. "No, actually, I'm from upstate New York. Buffalo area, wing capital of the world."

His wink has me laughing, and Lennon laughs from the backseat too just to mimic me. "So you've always been focused on food then, huh?"

"Truthfully, I went to college for business. Which I guess is good, since I started one. But my family is all still up there, running the largest chain of car dealerships in the region. It just wasn't for me."

His voice is tinged with something, but I leave it alone. Maybe I'm not the only one with baggage in this vehicle.

"President!" Lennon shrieks, pointing to a big white building that is most definitely not The White House.

I can't help the laugh that bubbles forth. "Ever since I told her we'd be moving back, she is obsessed that we live in the same town as the president. Not that I think she even knows half of what the president does or even who he is, but it's a selling point so I'll take it."

"Lennon, are you going to be president someday?" Jake yells to the back.

She claps her hands, her sweet baby noises still melting my heart. "Yes!"

"Believe me, she can do anything she sets her mind to. Like clogging the toilet with a baby doll, painting the rug in spaghetti sauce. She's really very talented." I reach my hand around the seat and tickle her legs, her loud belly laugh filling the car.

"It takes real talent." Jake nods soberly and pulls the car into a parking lot.

Looking up, my lips spread wide in jubilee. "You didn't."

"I did. One of the funnest places on earth, not to mention DC Come on, let's go."

Peering up at the building, I can't wait to get inside. I know Lennon is just going to love the Smithsonian National Zoo.

7

JAKE

The zoo had been a brilliant idea on my part, if I did say so myself.

Lots of meandering time to talk, cute animals to occupy the silent spaces, kid friendly, and great snacks along the way. All around, I'd planned a kickass date. And with my connections and some strings I'd greased and pulled, I'd gotten us up close and personal with the penguins, an activity that Lennon had loved.

I wanted to impress Samantha, but I also wanted to knock her socks off by how well I was treating her daughter. Not that my intentions were insincere; Lennon was truly cute and fun to be around, and her comments made me laugh my ass off. I don't think I'd ever gone out with a woman who had a child, much less taken one on a date with kid in tow. I'll admit I'd been intimidated leading up to it, but all in all, we'd done great.

Well, until Lennon had a major hissy fit in the elephant exhibit and all hell broke loose. I'd never seen a little body convulse like that, or a woman act so calm as a child ripped apart at the seams. I'd panicked, trying to calm her and compromise with her until Samantha shot me a look that said I'd better shut up or I'd lose my balls.

So I shut up and stood against the wall as Samantha stood by, her arms crossed over her perky chest, quietly speaking to Lennon as she wailed and whined. After a while, she'd picked her up, asked me to lead us to the car, and we hadn't said a word since.

The sun was just setting over the buildings as I pulled up in front of their high-rise, and my nerves were still unsettled. What I'd witnessed was real life shit, and I was just a bachelor looking to take a pretty woman on a date. It was a gutless move, but I stayed quiet, knowing that I wasn't this girl's father and honestly, I didn't really want to be.

I helped Samantha remove her things from my car, a relieved breath moving out of my chest as the realness moved out of my universe.

"Thank you for a fun day, I'm sorry about the ending." Her big, chocolate eyes regarded me apologetically as she held a sleeping Lennon in her arms.

I shifted uncomfortably, not sure how to say goodbye. This was awkward, and nowhere near how I hoped we'd be ending the night. Our conversation, banter really, had been great during the trip to the zoo. I learned more about her, she learned about me. By all accounts, it should have been a success. But ... here we were.

"Yeah," I rubbed the back of my neck. "Hopefully she'll be okay."

"Oh, she'll be fine." Samantha gave a small smile, and I think she felt the vibe that I couldn't handle this.

I felt like an asshole. Shooting out a hand, I weirdly rubbed her shoulder. "Well, have a good night."

Her head tilted and a strange expression came across her face before she turned and walked inside the glass doors.

Fuck me, I *rubbed* her shoulder. Who was I? Clearly all game had gone out the window due to a child's tears. I really was a prick.

I pushed open the door next to my apartment, and walked in, groaning as I saw that the Nationals were losing.

"Get off your knees ref, you're blowing the game!" Bryan shouted at the TV, a beer bottle in a hand appearing over the top of the leather couch.

The door slams shut behind me as I reach his fridge, grabbing a much-needed beer of my own. I grimace as I uncap it and take a swallow, my palette annoyed at the shitty suds of Bud Light sliding down my throat.

"You need better taste in beer." I sink down onto the leather lounger opposite the couch, and kick my brown Steve Madden slides off.

"*You* didn't seem to mind that shit when I was buying it for you senior year of college, ya cheap ass." Bryan doesn't even look over at me, his blond hair that usually hangs down past his shoulders was up in a ponytail.

"Yeah, well, I'll take anything tonight." I fisted a hand in my hair, sighing at the utter disaster that ended up being my date.

"Went that well, huh?" Finally, my best friend directs his eyes to me. And then sticks his hand down his gym shorts and scratches his balls.

"Nice, man, thanks for that. You're no better than a mangy dog."

"Is that why you kicked me out of the house?" He gave me his best puppy dog eyes.

I'd met Bryan my sophomore year of college, and we'd had that instant kind of friendship that hadn't waned or changed over the years. After school, we'd both stayed in the area, opting to get an apartment together. Now, it was my apartment. Once we'd hit thirty, we both agreed it was too weird and we made too much money not to have our own places. So Bryan moved into the one bedroom right next door, and things basically hadn't changed. Except now, I didn't have to put my headphones on when he was getting laid, and he didn't have to bitch at me about doing the dishes.

"I kicked you out because I thought having a bachelor pad would be cool, mostly. Now I barely use it to bring women home." I was sulking.

"So things with the single mom didn't pan out?" The smirk on his face was a little told-you-so backhand.

"Don't look so smug. It was going great … until her kid had a meltdown in the middle of an exhibit. I freaked, I don't know the first thing to do when it comes to children. She looked at me like I was such a major disappointment."

The sourness of Samantha's one eighty was still bitter in my mouth.

"Man, I told you not to go there. So she had a nice ass in college … doesn't mean you know a thing about her now. Usually I'm charming a woman and asking her where she hopes to travel throughout the world … not what color grapes her daughter likes. You were in way over your head, bud."

Maybe he was right. But it still sucked. "I guess you're right."

We drank our beer in silence for a while, and I tried to push past the failed attempt to take Samantha out. The Nationals scored a run, and Bryan clapped his hands.

"Oh well, it's over now. What should we do tonight?" I did not feel like going back to my apartment and thinking about how worthless I'd been.

Or why it was bugging me so much. It was one stupid date.

"I don't know ... McFlannery's?" Bryan shifted his eyes to me, raising a brow.

Our usual bar, just a block over, did not interest me tonight. "How about Jefferson Spy?"

We didn't normally frequent the showier nightclubs in the city, but I was feeling agitated. I needed to break out of my own head when I was this frustrated.

"The last time we went to the Spy, I brought home the freakiest chick, with one of the biggest bushes I've ever seen. Actually, it was kind of a turn on." Bryan tipped his beer back, finishing it.

"Dude, TMI."

"You know, I'm not really a man who requires grooming, or no grooming for that matter. I like 'em smooth, hairy, even with a little landing strip. I don't understand guys who discriminate. A woman is a woman, and I'd like to try all flavors."

He was babbling now, as my friend liked to do. Once he started, there usually was no shutting him up. But I had a short fuse tonight.

"So let's go out and I'll find you whatever type of pubic hair you're feeling tonight. Hell, it could even belong to a man since you sound so interested. Let's just go."

"Testy, are we? Sounds like somebody needs a good blow job."

I shake my head, laughing. "Are you offering?"

"Fuck you, go home." He finally rises off the couch, taking my empty bottle and his own and putting them in his recycling bin.

For a crude guy, Bryan was always obsessively neat. It's why he fit so well in his job at the Environmental Protection Agency.

"Fine, but pick me up in ten. We're going to the Spy."

8

SAMANTHA

"**M**om, are you sure you're okay with keeping her tonight?"

I put my cell phone on speaker, setting it down on the bathroom counter as I took a lock of my hair and ran the straightener through it. My inky long strands transformed from wavy curls to pin straight smoothness, and I loved the feeling.

"Honey, don't worry about it at all. We're going to make s'mores and watch movies, snuggle in my bed and then make pancakes in the morning. We're going to have a blast. You just have a good time."

My heart ached a little bit. I hadn't gotten a night on my own in probably ... well since Lennon had been born. She'd been with me every day since, a big issue to fight over when I'd been with Derek. I just didn't like to leave her, but I knew that at this point, a single mommy night out was much needed.

"Well, all right. Maybe I'll come over for breakfast with you two. I love you, Mom. Can you put Lennon on?" I took the time to layer two more coats of mascara on my eyelashes while I waited.

I heard some rustling in the background, and then a sigh.

"She's playing tea party right now, and it would be rude to leave her guests, or so she tells me. She loves you, Samantha. Go have fun, we will be fine."

Mom hangs up before I can protest, and suddenly my apartment feels too big and quiet without my daughter. Parenthood, a blessing and a curse all rolled into one. You weren't supposed to say things like that out loud, but I knew it was a huge blessing most of the time.

Looking at myself in the mirror, I assessed my face. Not too bad for overtired and overworked. The last two weeks had been busy but rewarding; I was finally sinking into my groove, Lennon had gone to her first week of preschool, but we couldn't get through the night without her climbing into my bed. One night, I'd accidentally set the fire alarm off and she'd had a complete meltdown, and it took me four hours to rock her to sleep.

I'd also dwelled unnecessarily on my failed date as the months changed and I didn't hear from Jake at all.

So when Jenna had asked if I wanted to grab a drink on Friday night, I took my opportunity to be a twenty-seven-year-old for once.

Except now, I was majorly considering taking off the skinny jeans and off-the-shoulder shirt I'd donned and instead getting in the bath. Bubbles up to my neck, a glass of wine and an erotic novel ... yeah, that might be a better night than a sweaty bar and strangers.

Sighing, because I'd given my word to Jenna, I went downstairs to call an Uber. If I was going out like a twenty-something, I was going to get drunk and need a taxi like a twenty-something.

"Hello," the driver greets me as I duck into the car ten minutes later. "Going to McFlannery's?"

"Yes, please." I knew of the bar, hadn't been there in a long time. Not since college. Resting my head against the seat, I watched Washington, DC fly past me in blurs of light.

All too soon, the car is pulling up outside the bar. I thank my driver and get out, standing on the curb waiting for Jenna. I send off a text to my mom, letting her know I arrived, and then a hand is on my arm.

"Hey, girl! You look great."

Jenna's blond hair brushes my cheek as she leans in for a friendly greeting, and I hug her back. She's dressed in a cute sundress, maybe too revealing for an early May night, but she looks amazing. Blue flowers dot the dress, and she's wrapped her golden locks into one of those sleek chignons that I can never pull off. Her blue eyes are lined with makeup, and she is easily the most gorgeous girl when we enter the bar.

"It's packed in here!" I couldn't help but swivel my gaze around the room.

"What have you, been living under a rock? No ... don't answer that. It's a yes, a Seattle rock. Don't worry girl, we'll get you back into the city life." She patted me on the back like I was some wounded duckling.

The grin that stretched my face was genuine, and I couldn't help but follow her as she commandeered two seats at the bar. The room teemed with people, energy and rock music bouncing off the walls. I let my body feel it, let the freeness of the night soak into my veins.

"Two tequila shots, and two Crown apples on the rocks." Jenna slammed her hand down on the bar as if telling the shaggy-looking bartender to hop to it.

I slid onto my stool. "Wow, you're not wasting any time, huh?"

"It's Friday night, time to let loose. Plus, we had a long week. God, I hate giving those reports, I'm so fucking glad it's over."

She shakes her head, not looking at me but at the men sitting around the bar.

"I think you're jaded from sitting in an office for so long. You need to go out and visit some of the parks." Part of the reason why I loved my job so much was that I knew where my efforts were going. I'd been in the parks, seen the good that could be done.

"Ew, bugs and dirt. No thank you!" The bartender sets our drinks down, and Jenna raises her shot glass to my own, signaling for me to up-end it.

I do, cringing before I tip it back and the tequila burns my throat. Instantly, I remember how much I hate this liquor, as the shivers and near-vomit feeling take me over. Coming up for air, I sputter and cough, grabbing the closest thing to me. Which just happens to be the apple-flavored whiskey on the rocks. I gulp it, coughing more as that burns too.

"Jeez, we need to train you a little better, huh?" Jenna's eyes sparkle with humor.

I finally catch my breath, straightening in my chair. "You work for the national parks, and you can't stand nature?"

She waves her hand as if to say whatever. "No one ever said you have to like your job. That's why it's a job. Now, which one do you think is cute?"

I look around us, checking out all of the men crowding the bar. Sure, there are some who peak my interest, but I'm so discouraged after the date with Jake that I'd rather just get drunk tonight.

"Count me out, but I'll be a great wing woman if you need me."

Jenna swivels her stool towards me. "Bad time with an ex?" Her eyes are all sympathy.

"Actually, no. Which is surprising, since my ex, Derek, and I were together for eight years. He gave me my daughter, Lennon,

I showed you her picture ... but by the end I think that we just didn't love each other. We weren't even friends to be honest, but the split was amicable."

"So then why the sourpuss? I have a long history of breakups and breakdowns, and if I'm out here trying to find 'The One,' or at least one for right now, then you should be too."

I sigh, taking another sip of my drink. The alcohol makes my veins buzz, and I kind of like it. "I had a pretty terrible date last month."

"Terrible as in, he picked you up on his bike and then cried at dinner while talking about his cat that just died? 'Cause yeah, that happened to me once."

I almost spit my drink I laugh so hard. "Okay well, not *that* bad. Although that sounds horrid! No, he acted like he could handle having Lennon come along with us, and at the first sight of tears, he couldn't have sprinted fast enough to get away from us. I get it, men our age are just starting to have kids, or have no interest in them at all. But come on, grow a sack. She's a toddler for fuck's sake. Part of me just wishes he wouldn't have even pretended to be okay with it in the first place."

Jenna nods solemnly. "That sucks, hon, I'm sorry. He's an idiot, but it doesn't mean there isn't someone out there who wouldn't be a nice match. Oh! We should get you on some dating apps."

I shiver, shaking my head. "Absolutely not. The guys on there are either looking to get between your thighs or into your bank account."

"That's kind of true. Okay, whatever. I'll flirt then, and you wing woman me!" Her voice was so optimistic, I had to chuckle.

While she flirted with the men around us, or plotted her next conquest, I quietly sipped my drink, surveying the bar. As hard as it was to leave Lennon, I had to admit that I'd needed this. The energy of the bar infused youth back into my veins, and made the problems untangle from my hair for just a few hours.

It was also hilarious to watch the mating activities of men and women trying to pick each other up. How it was initiated, who bought a drink for whom, how long it took before they were either making out on the dance floor or moving on to the next partner.

"Hey there." A cute blond slid up to Jenna, a beer bottle in his hand.

They started to talk, her giving off all of the body language that said, "I'm interested but not easy." I had to admit, girl knew how to play it.

"Do you want a drink, he's going to get us a round?" Jenna winked, her face turned towards me and away from him.

Not one to refuse a free drink, especially from someone I wasn't complicity agreeing to sleep with, I nodded. "I'll take a glass of white wine."

"I like your friend's style." Blond guy smiled, and I knew he was trying to score brownie points with Jenna by being nice to her friend.

Why did dating have to be this scoreboard of keeping track and counter moves? I was exhausted just watching it.

"Oh, here's my friend. This is Jenna and ... I'm sorry I never got your name." Blond guy ushers someone else up to the bar, and my first sip of wine tastes like sour grapes on my tongue.

"Jake." I can't help but spit his name out.

"Wait, your name is Jake? How funny is that ... although odd for a woman." Blond guy tips his head to the side.

"No, you idiot, her name is not Jake. Hi, Samantha." The brown-haired guy with the strong jaw and dimple in his cheek raises an awkward hand in greeting.

"No shit, you're Samantha. Nice to meet you, I'm Bryan." Jake's friend sticks his hand out for me to shake.

"Hi, nice to meet you." My mouth is dry as I shake his hand, my eyes trained on the guy who took me on a date and never called again.

"You two know each other?" Jenna looks way too excited about this possibility.

I can tell Jake is about to speak, his clover green eyes unsure of what to say, so I cut in. "We're old acquaintances from college. Good to see you again."

My tone is as normal as possible when the lie comes out, and I do it for Jenna's sake. I'm trying to have a fun night, be her wing woman, and I don't need any drama concerning our unsuccessful date and his allergy to children's temper-tantrums.

"So, what brings you girls out to McFlannery's?" Bryan breaks the tense silence.

"Well, we work together and I needed to get Samantha out, she just moved back to the city. How about you all?"

Jake sips on a beer and tries to stay behind Bryan, his eyes flitting to me every once in a while. This is ... weird and awkward. But I also can't keep my tipsy gaze off of him. He looks gorgeous; like a sparkly diamond of deliciousness in a bar full of rocks.

"We live in the building next door, not together though. We're far too established to be roommates." Bryan rolls his eyes and Jake chuckles quietly.

I sit on my stool, directing my attention elsewhere as Jenna and Bryan get deep into conversation. My night is suddenly dimmer, the alcohol feeling sluggish in my veins rather than giving me an upping kind of buzz.

And then he blocks my view of the other side of the bar. "I just wanted to come over and apologize for what happened last month."

Slim, toned arms gripping a glass of nearly clear liquid. Hair black as a midnight sky sweeping halfway down her back. Eyes lined with coal, shining in the dim light of the bar.

Samantha is practically edible, and here I am, making some lame-ass apology.

"Oh, Jake, it's not a big deal, really." She flips an errant strand of silky dark hair over her shoulder.

I move in closer when the couple next to us pushes me, my body coming dangerously close to hers. "I feel like an ass, so let me apologize. It wasn't cool of me to make you think that I was completely comfortable and calm with kids, even if Lennon is an awesome little girl. To be honest, I know nothing about kids, I'm basically the Simon Cowell of child rearing. And it wasn't cool not to call you after, even if it did go poorly. Which we both know it did."

I hoped my honesty was okay for her, because I couldn't be someone I wasn't. I couldn't stand here the entire night while Bryan macked on her girlfriend, pretending that we hadn't had a shitty date.

A smile peeks out from the corner of Samantha's mouth, and she takes the last sip of her white wine. "Jake ... thank you for the apology. It's nice to get some closure on it, but seriously, don't worry about it. We had one date, we never agreed to get married. I'm not looking for a father for Lennon. I'm not even looking for a boyfriend if it doesn't work out in my life right now. Seriously, you're off the hook."

Her amicable nature makes me release the breath I'm holding, and move the hands that were positioned in front of my nuts, just in case she decided to kick them. Believe me, I'd had it happen before when I was unnecessarily honest with a girl. Why was it that honesty got you a smack in the junk, while lying to some women kept them coming back for more?

"All right, good. So ... friends?" I shrug, holding out my hand.

"Such a lame peace treaty, but sure, why not?" Her mocha eyes sparkle.

"And since our friends seem to be minutes away from humping each other in the bathroom, how about I buy you a drink? I have a feeling you don't get the opportunity to come out by yourself much."

She scoots up on her stool, snorting as Jenna and Bryan get closer and closer to each other. "I rarely get time to shower by myself, so yeah, this is a total fluke. I'll take another glass of chardonnay, since you're offering."

And dammit, now I was picturing her in the shower. Long, slim body, water sluicing over that beauty mark on her face. I wonder if she had any other hidden beauty marks to find ...

Fuck. Get a hold of yourself, man.

I order her drink and try to keep a safe space between us, since my dick apparently loved the word friends and perked up even more when it was used in association with Samantha.

"So, did you have any ranger emergencies this week?" I smirk.

During our trip to the zoo, Samantha had filled me in a little more on what she does. And I'd teased her, like a typical guy trying to flirt, about how there definitely couldn't be anything more tame than being a park ranger in a national park.

"Actually, ya jerk, I did. We had a missing hiker in California, and I had to be in contact with the rangers there for forty-eight hours until we found her. Safely, thank God."

I nodded. "That's great, Samantha. I'm sure you're a force of nature in your job."

She giggled, sipping on her wine. "Was that a national park joke, Jake? So lame! Almost as lame as a fully grown man driving an ice cream truck around."

I put my hands over my heart like she'd shot me. "You wound me! My humor is almost as cold as my freezers though, it's true."

I ordered another beer, downing the third I'd been holding in my hand. McFlannery's felt different tonight, more *on* than it ever had been before. Or maybe it was just because I was sitting next to her.

"They aren't fucking in the bathroom yet, by the way. Should we separate them?" Samantha leans into me conspiratorially, and I almost swallow my tongue when she says the word fuck.

The word off her cherry lips makes my balls draw up tight, blood surging below my waist.

"Let the kids be kids." I wink, gulping down the new beer the bartender hands me.

"I haven't been here since college. Seems like ages ago ..." She swivels her head, trying to look at memories I can't see with my own eyes.

"I had some fun nights in this bar as a college kid. And a few drunken nights spent on the steps of the monuments that are a tad blurry." I laugh, remembering my own glory days.

"It's funny, I don't remember you from the fitness center. Did we ever talk?" Her wine glass is almost empty now.

It might be the beer, or the fact that she isn't looking at me with that "you spilled my daughter's milk" expression anymore ... but my tongue loosens.

"Well, I remember you. Always coming in wearing those spandex Madison shorts on, all legs and long hair. I think I said hi to you once as you came out of the locker room, and you gave me some fuck off smile."

Her mouth gapes. "You were checking me out, huh? Now I know you for the real stalker you are. Are you sure you didn't GPS my mom's address?"

"Cross my heart, hope to die. I'm just a gentle stalker."

She gives me a light-hearted side eye. "Yeah, okay, I'll buy it, but just this once. Don't worry about the fuck off smile, I was probably just pumping some Rick Ross in my headphones and it was getting me jacked up."

"He is the biggest boss, so I don't blame you."

We both smile, one of those moments where you were having a fun, bantering conversation but then neither person knew how to continue it.

"Should we all get out of here?" Samantha's blond friend, Jenna, I think, turns towards us for the first time in forty minutes.

I look at Samantha, her eyes unsure but confident at the same time. I'm not cocky enough to think she'll go anywhere with me, and I for once don't want to push my charm.

"We're actually going to stay here for another drink. But you two go ahead." I nod at Bryan, who winks over Jenna's head.

Why do I feel like I'm going to hear animal noises from the apartment next door tonight?

"You sure, Sam? I don't have to leave."

She places a hand on her friend's arm, and holds up two fingers on the other. "Wing woman's honor, I must not cock block. Go, I'll be fine. I'll Uber home and call you in the morning."

The two horny blonds leave, Bryan's hand practically down the back of her jeans before they're even out of the bar.

"Gosh, I miss that." Samantha sighs as she watches them go.

"What? Drunken hookups?" I snort, knowing Bryan's MO.

She hit my arm. "No! I guess, just the possibility of something new. The mysterious excitement. The newness of experiencing someone the first time."

The words out of her mouth made it sound fucking poetic, and suddenly I missed those things too. Even though I was sure I'd never felt them.

"Well, if you're looking for it, there is a rather decent piece of man meat right in front of you." I cheesily pointed to myself.

Her eyes squinted, like she was considering me, and her mouth puckered up.

"Hmm, okay. Yeah. Let's do this."

I swear, I almost choked. "Wha ... what?"

"It's my single night out, and I feel like doing something a little crazy. I know you're only a gentle stalker, which is okay on my list, and you are pretty nice to look at. So, are you going to take me home?"

I don't know what God I had to get down on my knees for and thank, but I promised myself I'd do it tomorrow. I'd cut off my right hand in some Pagan sacrifice if that's what it took to be rewarded with this one night, this one moment, right here.

Grabbing her hand, I started running from the bar with her in tow. Samantha's tinkling laugh filled my ears.

"Quick, let's get you upstairs before I turn back into a pumpkin, or however that Disney movie goes."

"First he drives an ice cream truck, and now he's quoting Disney movies. You sure you're not just a big kid yourself?"

Flinging open the door to my building, I turn for a split-second and face her. "Oh, you'll see *just* how big I am."

Giggles fall on my ears as I impatiently jam the buttons for the elevator.

10

SAMANTHA

Our connection was a mix between him leading me to his apartment, frantic kissing, hysterical laughing, and clumsy movements fueled by alcohol.

When we finally made it inside his door, he waved his hand around. "Welcome to my humble abode."

I surveyed the place, bachelor the only word coming to my mind, but at least it was clean. A medium-sized two bedroom with an open concept; his bedroom out of sight, the living room space in the middle, and a kitchen on the other end. Moderate furnishings, decent light, some personal affects ... it was nice.

But I wasn't here to talk, or examine the decor. Boldness and a dry spell compelled me forward, into his arms. My mouth found his, our lips meeting and greeting. I navigated his mouth, his tongue, testing the pressure of his nibbles and reveling in the tiny bites he was laying along the seams of my mouth.

"Did you want a glass of wine or something?" Jake breathed between kisses, his body pressing mine into the wall by the front door.

"You already locked down the sale, I don't need an after-drinks drink." I pushed the hem of his T-shirt up, feeling the smooth, hot skin beneath.

The excitement at my fingertips traveled south, sending a jolt between my legs. Jake's fingers moved up and into my hair, massaging my scalp as his tongue danced with my own. Sensation covered me everywhere, making my flesh hypersensitive.

"Then let me take you to the bedroom part of this tour. Please keep all hands inside the vehicle—"

I snorted before shutting him up with my mouth again. He moved us, swaying and circling me towards his queen-sized bed. I was too tipsy to notice if it was made or not, but it smelled all right and I was horny, so my judgment zipped its lips.

It had been a long, dry spell ... almost like the Sahara Desert of sex droughts. Even though I'd had a boyfriend, it had been eight long months without action, and too many nights of using my own fingers while pretending to take a bath.

Once in his darkened bedroom, I sit down on the bed, my hands on Jake's hips as he stares down at me like he's about to make a meal of my body. A shudder of anticipation runs along my spine, and I quickly toe out of my heels, sending them across the room with a kick. That must spur him, because all of a sudden he's gently pushing me back and climbing over me.

"Ah, do you know the fantasies I had about freshman you?" He pushes a lock of hair behind my ear, and it felt more intimate than the dirty fuck I had in mind.

"Please, show me." It was a half-joke, half-plea.

In one fell swoop, he pulled his shirt off using one hand to grab the material from behind his head.

"You've got to be kidding me. That is some Magic Mike shit." I couldn't help but laugh as he bit my neck.

"Stay tuned for the show, baby." Jake stood, and I swallowed my humor.

Abs running across a long, tapered torso danced in my gaze.

Strong shoulders, the kind you could hang onto in case of flood or famine, or very rough sex, gave way to arms that had definitely been worked on at the gym. His hair was mussed where my hands had been playing in it, and I could make out the smattering of hair that dipped below the sightline of his belt.

"Unbutton your pants." His voice wasn't joking anymore, and my arousal shot through the roof.

I flicked the button on my jeans, the hiss of my zipper resonating in the air. Slowly he bent down, picking up my legs that were hanging off the side of the bed. His fingers met my bare feet, tickling and sending licks of fire up my thighs. Jake pulled, the look on his face lethal, and I shimmied my jeans as he pried them off. Past my hips they went, revealing the blush pink cotton thong I had on. And all the way down, until Jake was throwing them to the floor beside him.

"God damn, Samantha ..." He bit his lip, still standing in front of me, not touching a part of my body but making me wet anyway.

"Are you going to show me those fantasies, or not?" My voice was a croak, and I realized that the panting in my ears was my own.

I wasn't usually this impulsive, but the past six months of my life had laughed in my face and showed me that apparently, I *could* be a daredevil. I'd dared to leave Seattle, breaking off a relationship with the only man I'd ever loved in search of something more, something that would grab me by the hair and make me feel alive. I'd dared to take a new position, one that I'd never dreamed of attaining. I'd dared to show my daughter how a boss female was supposed to act. I'd dared to become a single mom, and figure out all the details of my life on my own.

And now I was daring to hook up with the hot semi-acquaintance that I'd gotten off on the wrong foot with. It wasn't perfect, but it sure was sexy and freeing. The Samantha who once was would have never done something this irresponsible; normally, I would have gone home early to my mother's and snuggled up with Lennon. But something about this night, something about this year and being home, something about this man ... it all felt right in a cosmic sort of way.

Kind of like when your horoscope revealed the exact thing you were looking for. They always knew, those astrology gods.

His grin was cocky as he moved over me, his hands landing on either side of my head as I scooted back on the mattress. I wrapped my legs around his waist, shamelessly grinding my pelvis against his as he settled between my thighs.

"You have no idea how good this feels." I felt my eyes rolling back in my head.

"I can make it feel better."

A hand snakes down my bare shoulder, onto my stomach where my shirt has risen up, and kneads my hip. Tiny sizzles of electricity shoot straight to my clit, the blood pumping and making me squirm. And then his blunt finger tips are pushing past the thin boundary of my underwear, and moving down, trapping his hand between us.

"Yes, yes ... God, yes." I'm loud, I know it, but I can't help it.

I haven't had a man's hands on me in far too long, and Jake knows how to use his as he strokes my wetness, swirling it around my core and then plunging a finger inside. So close, he had me right there so quickly, the ball of nerves bunching close and winding so tight ...

"Oh my God!"

White bursts at the edge of my vision, Jake's fingers pressing down on the button that was making my entire body shake with ecstasy.

"Wow, I think that's a new record for me." His deep voice growled in my ear, and I could feel just how big he was as his hard-on pressed through his jeans and onto my thigh.

I had to catch my breath, the orgasm taking a toll on my entire system. "It's been a while."

Jake worked on the buttons on my top, his green eyes staring at my face as he worked. "I can't even imagine why. At the risk of being seriously corny, I would devour you every single night."

His words didn't make me laugh, but made me blush. And made me want more. While he worked on my shirt, I reached down for his belt, struggling to free it as he laid on top of me.

"Can you just get naked already?" I couldn't work his pants off.

"I thought you'd never ask." Jake stood up again, and I took the opportunity to rid myself of my bra and thong.

While I wasn't a spring chicken, I had made a human with my body, I thought I looked pretty good. Aside from my C-section scar, I'd never been particularly shy when it came to my body. And apparently, Jake liked what he saw.

"Jesus ..." His eyes burned in the dim light of the apartment, nothing but the hall light near the door illuminating us.

Keeping those green orbs glued to my body, he pushed his pants and boxers down as one, his cock springing free and proudly bobbing as it jutted from his body. I tracked its movements as he walked to his bedside table, pulling a condom from it and rolling it on. He was big, thick and hard as a steel pipe.

I couldn't wait to have him inside me.

My core throbbed as he tracked me, the primal scent in the air like some kind of jungle. I almost giggled, but the need for him to get on this bed and fuck the living shit out of me was too strong. I could feel myself squirming, my nipples knotting.

"God damn," Jake's growl hisses in my ear as he enters me.

His cock plunges deep, his hips meeting mine and driving me into the bed. My walls mold around him, my legs spreading wide and then wrapping around his hips. I can't control the moan that bursts from my mouth, the feeling so exquisite that I can't help but close my eyes and relish it for a few seconds.

"You feel ..." I can't even finish the sentence.

His eyes meet mine, our faces pressed close as he starts to move, slowly at first and then deeper, harder. I grip those shoulders that are the perfect anchor, moving my hips up to meet him on every down stroke.

"I want to see your body move."

In one flash second, Jake is rolling us over, perfectly positioning me on top, his dick spearing me from the inside. It's like a perfect porn move, one I never thought was possible, and I can't help but grin at his cocky smirk as he grips my waist, moving me ever so slightly.

"You're really pulling out the big moves, huh?" I couldn't help but grind on him, my clit pressing against him in the most delicious way.

"I just really wanted to do this." His big hands move to my breasts, rolling and pinching my nipples in a move that has jolts spiraling to my core.

"Keep doing it." I plant my hands on his chest, tilting my head to the ceiling and taking control.

"That's it, ride me, Samantha." His voice is a prayer, a command.

I follow instructions at my own rhythm, working everything out on him, taking my pleasure without asking a thing. My legs shake, my hands grip the sexy hair running down Jake's happy trail, and I keep moving myself up and down on him, his hardness hitting every single spot that makes me see stars. My toes curl, and the heat licking down my spine has me chasing that ever elusive combustion.

All of a sudden, my breasts are smashing into his chest, my chin fitting right down in the crook of his neck. I'm trapped, unable to move.

"What ..."

"Feel the way I have the control now?" One hand bound my wrists behind my back, tight enough to where I couldn't break free, but loose enough to know he was playing a sexy little game.

I'd never been much into anything kinky, I'd only ever slept with one person before Derek and everything had been ... well, vanilla.

In just a matter of seconds, I'd learned that there was nothing vanilla about Jake Brady.

"Let me move you, Samantha." His other hand, strong and firm, gripped my ass, the fingers tapping on my right butt cheek as he moved my hip for me.

I could barely speak I was so turned on, the struggle of letting him have control and fighting for every tiny sliver of sensation was making my heart pound out of my chest. His hand locked around my wrists, my entire body flush against him, submitting to the will of his hands.

"Yes ... please ..." My words were nonsensical, the way he'd taken over everything swamping me with a hazy lust.

"You're going to come again? Let me feel it, because you're about to make me come ..." His jaw tics as my body grinds on top of him.

Who had the control now?

His declaration makes me sprint over that cliff again, my orgasm slamming into me. My limbs go rigid and then lax with wild abandon, every ounce of ecstasy washing over me.

"Right there ..." Jake bucks up into me, his movements making my pleasure go on and on and on.

He lets out a feral growl, his hold on my ass gripping tighter while he hurls my body down onto him, holding it while his muscles tense and contract, and then repeating the motion. My vision feels hazy as I tilt my head to watch him, the gorgeous,

Adonis-like quality of him making my heart pound a little harder.

Heaving a sigh as I burrow more into his chest, I let the aftershocks of a second glorious orgasm wrack my body. Jake's arms come around me, his cheek pressed to the crown of my head.

We stay like that for a long time, until sleep steals over my consciousness. And I drift peacefully, thinking that I got what I truly needed, and perhaps something I wasn't looking for.

11

S tevie Wonder's "Living for the City" fill the air as I stretch my arms over my head.

Which is pounding. I blink open an eye, the light of day instantly zapping my retina and making me want to climb into whatever blanket cocoon I can manage. Don't believe anyone when they tell you that you can drink the same amount you once did in college ... because this side of a hangover at twenty-seven feels like I got run over by a dump truck.

"Oh, *good morning*, sunshine."

The end of the bed suddenly becomes heavy, and everything that happened last night comes rushing back at me. Jake, the bar, too many glasses of wine, sex. Great sex, orgasm-inducing sex. I stretch my legs out, remembering the post-ache of great sex that I haven't felt in far too long.

"Are you one of those dreaded morning people?" I don't peek my eyes out for fear of the sun.

Strong hands grip my legs under the blanket, and a flash of his hands on me last night has my body tingling even in its tired state.

"You know it. I got in a run around the monuments this

morning and then came back to make you breakfast. You can thank me later." Jake's cheery voice invades my blanket fort, and I peek my head out.

Sure enough, he sits on the edge of the bed in running shorts. And that's it. Just running shorts.

My tongue almost spills out of my mouth, because damn I guess I hadn't been able to fully see him in the sex haze of last night. He was a gorgeous specimen, with long toned arms and a six-pack sprinkled with just the sexiest amount of hair. Beads of sweat still clung to his happy trail, and that was getting every part below my waist *very* happy again.

And then my stomach growled.

He chuckled. "Looks like I didn't make that breakfast a second too soon. Come on, there's bacon."

Sitting up, the sheets pooled around me and I am suddenly aware that I was naked. Very, very naked. "Um, do you have like ..."

I trailed off when his gaze seemed to linger on me, his green eyes turning molten emerald. Jake cleared his throat, his dimple coming out as he smirked. "Let me get you a T-shirt."

"I don't have to stay ..." We'd hooked up, this wasn't a thing.

At least I didn't think it was. We'd had one bad date, an honest conversation about how he wasn't looking to be a father and I wasn't looking to supply Lennon with one, and then we'd done the horizontal hula. That didn't mean he had to make me eggs.

"I want you to stay." His simple sentence was said with a shrug.

That adorable look on his face, paired with a body I could, and had, licked from head to toe, weakens my resolve.

"I know what was said last night but ... I want to spend time with you, Samantha. I don't want to just screw each other's brains out and then high five when you walk out the door. Although, that sounds really nice. But, no, I do want more. And that may be more than you were looking for when you booty-dragged me out of that bar, and we don't know each other that well, but I like you. We can go slow, see where this goes."

He was right, I wasn't looking for a hookup buddy. To be honest, I barely had time to paint my nails, much less meet someone for casual sex. I also didn't really have time to date, but there was a spark between us that I hadn't found in a long time. Some unspoken thing that we just *had*, and I had to admit that when he'd asked me out the first time, I knew instantly that I'd explore it.

"I think I can do that. That is ... if you made the eggs sunny side up." I got out of the bed in all my naked glory.

His eyes fell down my body, which wasn't perfect, but was still okay in my eyes. I had stretch marks on my boobs and a faded C-section scar from where they'd taken Lennon out. My legs were toned from chasing around a three-year-old, and I thanked good genes for my thick hair and slim arms.

Self-consciously, I put my hands over the scar at the bottom of my stomach.

"Don't do that, you're beautiful. Honestly, I think it's kind of sexy."

I rolled my eyes. "Okay, what are you, Mr. Perfect? Your sweetness is going to make me gag."

"Well, don't go that far yet ... because I scrambled the eggs." He walks across the apartment to the kitchen, my eyes following his ass the entire time.

I go to his dresser and grab a T-shirt for myself, my comfort level in his place surprising me. I follow him, my mouth salivating for a cup of coffee. And to my delight, a steaming mug is sitting on the small table near his counter space.

"Ah, the nectar of the gods ..." I dove straight for it, taking a huge gulp and feeling my system kick somewhat back into gear. "What time is it anyway?"

Jake chuckles, loading two plates with breakfast food and bringing them over. "Coffee addict, huh? It's about nine."

"You get up before nine on a weekend? Why? There is no one jumping in your bed, or begging you for donuts." I fold my legs underneath me and revel in the newness of this.

It feels comfortable but strange all at the same time, eating breakfast with a man who I'm just getting to know. *Intimately.* That makes me blush internally.

"How do you know that I'm not jumping on my own bed, demanding donuts? Or that Bryan isn't doing so?" He points his fork at the wall, indicating Bryan's place just on the other side.

The playlist switches to "Fire and Rain" by James Taylor, and I tap my foot to the classic song. "Touché. Pretty good playlist you have going there, Jake."

"I'm an ice cream and music connoisseur, what can I say?" He smiles around a forkful of eggs.

"And so humble about it," I tease him, finishing my coffee, and holding out the mug. "More please."

"Should I just bring you the pot?" His foot hits mine under the table, and a warming sizzle of Saturday morning bliss spreads over me.

"That would probably be beneficial to all involved. Do you have to work today?" I wasn't sure what kind of hours he kept.

"I don't, which is rare. There aren't any major events this weekend, although I could probably make a good chunk of change if I parked the truck on the national lawn today. But I have to give myself some days off. I employ a few drivers who will make the rounds to the neighborhoods tonight, but I'm playing hooky on this beautiful Saturday. How about you, any plans?"

I finish my plate and rest my elbows on the table, admiring

the way the light makes his hair a dark golden color. "Lennon slept over my mom's house, and I was actually supposed to go over there for breakfast."

"Oh shit, do you need to go?" His expression changes to one of guilt.

I lay a hand over his, liking the way it feels under my palm. "Relax. If I needed to get somewhere, I would just go. I think you know by now that what you see is what you get with me, I'm not going to sugarcoat."

"And I particularly like that about you, you know." Jake scoots closer, clearly abandoning our food.

He wraps his arms around my waist, his T-shirt rising up past my hips. Fingers making circles on my skin, sending shock-waves of memories of last night through my system. Leaning in, I press my lips to his, basking in the sheer spontaneity of what was happening.

"Do you think Jenna is over at Bryan's?" The thought popped into my head and past my lips.

Jake let out a loud laugh. "I made you breakfast and am trying to seduce you over it, and you're thinking about your friend getting laid."

I had to crack up too. "Sorry, I was just wondering!"

"We could go check if you want to? Although, I've walked in on my fair share of Bryan's female friends, and now that I have my own place, I'd like to avoid that as much as possible. But for you, anything."

I scoot back into him. "Nah, let's get back to that seduction over the breakfast table before I have to leave."

"I could even pull a Bull Durham and spill a gallon of milk if that would be sexy to you?"

My giggle was swallowed by Jake's mouth, and then there was no more laughing matter.

12

The sun peeked over the top of the Jefferson Memorial as my feet pounded the concrete of the Tidal Basin, early morning runners jogging in packs around the popular tourist trap.

Except this early in the morning, six a.m. to be correct, it is still a place for the residents of this city. A quiet, treaty-like calmness falls over the two mile loop, all of the regulars who use this trail to exercise forming a pact not to disturb the peace.

I've been running it for five years now, ever since I realized that if you don't work out after college and only drink beer, that you'll get a gut. It's a morning routine, one that gets me out of my head and also keeps me in shape. What no one told men was that they had a little anxiety attack when they turned thirty as well, it wasn't just women. I'd hit that milestone birthday and wanted to rewind time to when I was eighteen, hanging out in the local Applebee's parking lot trying to pick up girls.

My phone beeped, and I slowed to a walk, coming to the end of my second loop, the sweat from the humid morning making my shirt cling to my back.

Dad: *I hope we can count on you to come home for the grand opening of the new dealership.*

Annoyance burns along with exhaustion in my veins, and I shove my phone back into the armband I wear. It dings again, the sound coming through my earbuds. If I just turn my music back on and plow through another loop, will they go away?

Michael: *Dad wants you to come up for the opening of the Utica dealership, and we all think it would be nice for you to be here.*

I want to tell my brother to fuck off, but it would only make them more annoyed. And it's not like they understand anyway, they never have. My two brothers never left the family womb, going right into the family business after earning their associate's degrees. My sister left briefly for college, and then she and her husband moved back, Hugh taking a position within the family fold. My stepmother did the books for the Buffalo dealership, and some of my cousins worked on the sales floor.

They didn't accept my decision to break out on my own, to try and make something for myself in a city that I loved and felt at home in. Even after I'd drawn up my business plan for Cones & Corks, and started to become really successful, they still treated my business like a hobby or something that was impermanent.

My mom would understand if she were still alive. The thought wasn't a new one, but it still stung as I headed down through the Franklin Delano Roosevelt Memorial, smiling as a dog that someone was walking barked at the fake statue sitting next to our thirty-second president. Even though she'd died when I was ten, I remembered how she'd encouraged my dreams, all of the imaginations of a little boy lighting up her smile.

Jake: *Maybe, I have to see if I can secure drivers for that weekend. Summer is very busy for my business, as you know.*

I typed the answer back, walking the blocks towards my apartment and stopping for a large cup of Compass Coffee. While I was at it, I took my phone out again.

Jake: *Hope your morning is going well, beautiful.*

Staring at the screen, I will her to type back. I know she's busy, but I'm not used to not being able to see a woman I'm, well, I guess courting was the word but it sounded so stiff. Samantha's unattainableness kind of makes her more attractive to me, but it's starting to become more frustrating than it is a game of mystery. We haven't been able to see each other in a week and a half, not since she slept at my place. And rocked my fucking world.

I'm jiggling the key in the lock of my apartment, my cock hardening thinking about plunging into her sweet folds on the chair in my kitchen, when she finally texts back.

Samantha: *Sorry, got oatmeal in my hair, had to wash it again before leaving.*
Jake: *Why are you apologizing? How is the rugrat?*

Our interactions for the past ten days have consisted of text and picture messages, with a few funny memes thrown in. I especially like to send her Leslie Knope GIFs to tease her about her job. And I've been trying to ease into the subject of her daughter after our disastrous first date, and after basically telling her at McFlannery's that I wasn't looking for responsibility or fatherhood.

Because ... maybe I'd change my tune if it meant I could

spend more time with her. I mean, I was good with kids, I knew how to handle them ... kind of? Samantha was sexy and capable, a real woman, and I was thinking it was time for this bachelor to, excuse my language, shit or get off the pot. Spending that night with her, her soft, natural body under mine, flipped a switch in my brain. I had the business, I loved my city ... but I needed more. I probably had for a while, but had been wasting my time with recent college graduates and girls who were nearly certifiable.

Samantha: *She's good, babbling about baby dolls this morning and asking why their heads can pop off but not hers. The things that come out of that little girl's mouth. How was your run?*

Jake: *Tell her you could try, if she wants. Or that if she's not good, Santa will pop her head off. Run was good, nice morning down by the monuments. You should join some time.*

Samantha: *That's not how the whole "behaving well for Christmas" threat works, but good thought. Believe me, you don't want company. The one and only time I tried to take Lennon on a run with me, she threw her juice box at a stranger walking past the stroller, and then tried to escape as I apologized profusely.*

Jake: *HA! My kind of kid, person probably gave her a stink eye. So, do you think you'll be able to get out for a date this week?*

Samantha: *Depends, are you asking me out on a second date? I thought I scared you off the first time.*

Jake: *I mean, if you wanted to get naked again, we could just do that. But I thought I'd actually treat you to dinner, since yes, I'd like to take you on a date.*

I started the shower, hoping she would agree. Thinking that the third time might be the charm, since our first date ended in tears and the "second" finished ... well, inside her, I really wanted to show her just exactly what something between us could look like. I could sense, when I'd put her in a cab on the sidewalk of my building the morning after our sex session, that she wasn't considering me a serious bet. And while I knew that this body and hair and dimple could make me seem like just another fuckboy—I was very humble—there was also substance behind this pretty face.

Why now? Why this woman? I didn't know, but I wasn't going to fight it. I'd learned, from my family especially, that I couldn't fight or fake something I wanted, or I'd be miserable in life.

Samantha: *I suppose I could ask for a prison furlough on Saturday night...*

Jake: *Tell your warden I'll buy her a lollipop. One of those big rainbow ones. And I'll let her ride around in the ice cream truck.*

Samantha: *You know that kind of makes you sound like the kind of strangers I tell her not to take candy from ...*

Jake: *Very funny. I'll pick you up at seven?*

Samantha: *I'll be the one with oatmeal in my hair.*

Plugging my phone in to charge, I jumped in the shower.

And may have taken a little extra time with my hand under the hot spray imagining the curvy brunette who'd ridden me like I was her prized stallion. Showing up to the office half an hour late didn't matter when you were the boss.

13

SAMANTHA

Finally, she was down. Four Oreos and a glass of red wine sat on the coffee table, and the second season of Game of Thrones was cued up on the TV.

So what, I was the only person not completely enthralled in the seventh season? Some of us had to work ... and hadn't realized how hot Jon Snow was until recently so they began bingeing just to see his beautiful face. Sue me.

It was my night of relaxation. One of those rare times when Lennon went to sleep early with no fuss, and I got to be a Netflix-surfing, Instagram-stalking, junk food-eating creature camped out on my couch. I actually lived for these moments of guilty pleasures and peaceful ignorance of the issues of my world.

So it would figure that the minute I sat down, my charcoal face mask just beginning to harden, that my phone would ring.

"Ughhhh!" I made an annoyed sound, not too loud as to not wake the sleeping little girl in the next room, but enough to let my frustration out.

Staring at the screen, I saw a familiar face. One that made

me smile, and my annoyance at getting a late start in Westeros subsided.

"Well hi there!" I picked up the FaceTime call, the black cream on my face scary and hilarious.

"Oh I see that when you move to the East Coast, beauty just goes right downhill."

Lila, my best friend from Seattle, chirped back happily from the other end of the connection. Her short blond hair curled around her shoulders in that edgy, artistic way every girl could pull off back on the West Coast. Her blue eyes sparkle with sarcasm as we look at each other for the first time in months.

"Sorry I've been so damn busy. Work has been ... exhausting but great. And between that and making sure the little princess is living the life, I basically just sleep whenever I can."

She settles back into her couch, and from what I can see of her condo, not much has changed. A pang of homesickness for Seattle hits me. I had some wonderful times there, an entire life and family of friends and coworkers.

"Okay I can forgive you, but just this once. Plus, I need a place to stay when I decide to visit, so I guess we will have to stay friends. How is my favorite little brat?"

Lila was my go-to babysitter whenever I needed her, and she was the one I spent most weekends with. She'd accompany Lennon and I to the park or the mall; she was there for my daughter more than Derek was. I knew they missed each other, because Lila would often text me silly selfies to show to Lennon during the week.

"She's good, loving having my mom around and she really likes her preschool. Except the other day she came home telling me she learned the F-word, but that she couldn't tell me what it meant. I told her that just this once, she could tell me. Lila, my heart was pounding so fast, I was not prepared. And you know what she said to me?"

Her smile is expectant. "What did she say?"

I have to swallow a laugh. "She got all quiet, and then she goes ... Fagina. FAGINA! I swear to God, I almost bust out laughing. I was so fucking thankful she didn't say fuck."

The phone jumbles a bit as the screen swings, and Lila's cackles fill the air. "Oh my God, you almost just made me pee. That is too freaking hilarious. That's my girl."

I pick up my glass of wine, not able to resist the beautiful scarlet that will numb my thoughts soon. "So what's up with you? How's the hospital? Any boy updates?"

She sighs. "The hospital is good, babies always gotta be born and I'm the one holding mama's hand. Ugh men, but definitely more like boys. The last date I went on, the guy drove a crotch rocket and expected me to ride with no helmet, in a mini skirt. I didn't even make it to dinner, I refused to go more than a mile when I swallowed a bug."

I cringed but laughed. "Oh lord, why do some of these guys even exist? At least you're still bringing tiny humans into the world. It feels like just yesterday you were reaching between my thighs and pulling that screaming girl out."

It's true, I'd met one of my best friends in Seattle because she was my labor and delivery nurse. We bonded over our hate of *Everybody Loves Raymond*, the only thing on the hospital TV for eight hours of my labor, and hiking. She'd seen some of my inspirational pictures that I'd planned out in a book to help me through birth, and we had gotten to chatting on which trails we liked best.

And out of a love for mountains, a hatred of a comedian, and the fact that we had both intimately seen my vagina, a friendship was born.

"Why are you so obsessed with me seeing your va-jay-jay? It looks just like any other, so don't expect me to go telling you that you have some perfect puss. What's up with you on the guy front? Has douche-nozzle contacted you?"

Lila knew the ins and outs of my breakup with Derek, and had been instrumental in helping me leave him. She wasn't a friend who would stand by diplomatically and let me make mistake after mistake, she actually spoke her mind when it came to the tough stuff. I really valued that.

"Yes, *Derek* has contacted me, but only to cancel multiple visits to see Lennon. I'd never say this in front of my daughter, but God, I could kill the man. Sometimes I envision dunking him face first into a vat of Tabasco, just to see his eyes burn."

"Brutal yet delicious, love it. And fuck him, seriously, fuck him and his hippie, free to the world attitude. Man up, grow a sack, and take care of your kid. Moving on though, any hot boy action over there on Capitol Hill?"

I don't know if I should mention Jake. It seems too soon to be dating someone, but that *is* what I'm doing. And I like him; he's sexy and nice and doesn't make things awkward even with our hiccups. Plus, the one person I *can* talk to this about is Lila, so I might as well go for it.

"Soooo, I'm kind of ... seeing someone."

A piece of chocolate stops halfway into her mouth, and she drops it. "No fucking way! I didn't think you'd actually answer in that way! Shit, I'm so involved already. Tell me everything!"

I laugh, settling more into my couch. I miss this girl time, to giggle like high schoolers and gossip.

"Okay, well ... it's actually funny because we knew each other. Sort of. He worked in the fitness center when I was in college, and apparently used to check me out. Which, duh, makes me feel like I still have my freshman year ass and that does all kinds of things for your confidence. His name is Jake, he's thirty and owns his own food truck business here. He's really successful, and he's one of those people that you can tell likes their job ... like actually doesn't mind waking up and doing work all day because he's in love with it. Which I didn't know I thought was sexy, but oh my God does it make the panties a little damp."

Lila fans herself. "Super, super hot. Responsibility makes my nipples hard these days."

"We went on a first date and he asked if Lennon could come along, which ended up being a disaster and almost derailed the whole thing. But then I saw him at this bar the other week, and I ended up going back to his place."

"Tell me there was sex. Please, God say you had sex with a man." She bites her nails.

"I had sex with a man. Great sex. Mind blowing sex. Best sex I've probably ever had, although when you've only been with three guys is that saying much?"

"If your toes were curling and you were worshipping the orgasm gods, then yes, you can claim it." She nods sagely.

"I worshipped them all right, worshipped them more than once. Anyway, afterward he was super sweet, and he made me breakfast the next morning, and now we've been talking for about two weeks over text and short calls."

My best friend sighs like a love-sick puppy. "God, I am so jealous and proud at the same time."

I chew on my lip. "But ... part of me doesn't know. It's not just me I have to worry about, and it seems so soon to be dating after Derek. He's already had a blip on the perfection scale when it comes to Lennon, and I don't know ... I never want to corner someone into becoming a parent. And that's what he's signing up for if we get serious. Part of me really likes him, but part of me also is scared shitless because who the hell would want to take on this much baggage?"

There is silence as I watch her eyes assess me. "Okay, I'm hearing you on the scary feelings, but ... isn't it his call whether or not he wants to take all of that on? And you should not feel guilty for anything, because I know that is where some of this is coming from. You were in love, and had a child who is one of the coolest little chicks on the planet. This Jake guy clearly is into you, because he keeps coming back, and we all know that if a guy wants to be with you, he'll make it work. Nothing about you is going to turn him away, he's already seen it all and clearly, he likey. So stop doubting it. Live a little, have hot sex, be adored. You deserve it. You don't need to think about marriage or forever right now, just let things flow and see where they go."

My stomach dipped, because I knew she was ultimately right. It was like ever since I'd had Lennon, my attitude on men shifted directly to marriage and long term whenever one came into the picture. But I didn't have to find a husband, I was doing just fine on my own. It was just my messed-up mommy hormones, or more likely society, that told me I needed to pair off and find a mate.

"And he owns a food truck goddammit, indulge your hot chef fantasy a little. Lick chocolate off his abs. Oh God, he has abs, doesn't he?"

"Six individual ones I can trace with my tongue." I wiggled my butt at being so sassy.

"Fuck, I'm so jealous. Enough about you, jeez Samantha. Can we discuss the *Real Housewives of New York* because I am dying without our Wednesday night wine dates!"

I was all too happy to delve into trashy TV talk with her, my anxiety about Jake calmer than it was just hours ago.

The sounds of *Beauty and the Beast* rang out from the living room, Lennon's off key singing both adorable and grating.

"Okay, so I'm definitely going with this one." I look at my mother as I stare at my own reflection in the floor length mirror.

After emptying out literally my entire closet, I've settled on a simple blue and white striped wrap dress with tan wedge sandals. It's cute, but dressy enough if Jake is springing for a fancy place.

"You look gorgeous, sweetie. But ... I thought you said it didn't go well with Jake before. Although, I'm not sure how, since he's so handsome, Samantha. And he's always so nice with the neighborhood kids."

I rolled my eyes, my previous words to my mother working against me. Wasn't that always how it went?

"I'm still ... testing the water. He's nice, and funny, and it's nice just to be looked at like I'm a woman and not a diaper-bag carrier or warm body who sleeps beside him."

"I won't say I told you so ... but I told you in year four of your relationship with Derek that if you had no ring by that time, the man was never going to marry you. Never give up the milk before he buys the cow."

My mother nods to herself sagely, as if she hadn't just related my vagina and sex to a barn animal. But I couldn't argue, she was right. And she'd agreed to come over and watch Lennon for a few hours while I pretended to be a normal single person, so I had to remain cordial.

My heart and head still flip-flopped between good idea and bad idea on this whole date with Jake thing. When I'd gone back to his place after the bar, it had been a spur of the moment, one-night stand type of deal. Sure, it helped that I'd had a banter with him beforehand, and was a semi-stranger after apparently seeing him in the college gym ... but after the first date I was so sure there wasn't going to be a second. I guess some people were right when they said a magical cock could change how you felt about a man.

"Mommy, when I grow up, I want to be Lumière!" Lennon ran in, dancing around with nothing but her big girl underwear on.

We'd been having trouble with potty-training, but she was finally starting not to have accidents during the day. And if I promised to buy her pink butterfly undies, she was even better.

Also, great ... my daughter's biggest goals were to become a talking candlestick.

"You can be whatever you want to be." I kissed the top of her head, knowing that there was no way in hell she could be a singing inanimate object, but that discussion was for another day.

The buzzer to the door rang, and I hesitated as to what I should do. I'd taken a leap inviting Jake into Lennon's life at the first chance, and it hadn't paid off well. All of the parenting books, and apps and opinionated Facebook moms would advise against inviting strange men into your children's lives until you're completely sure and serious about continuing a relationship.

But ... I'd always done parenting my way, and my daughter wasn't completely screwed up so I must be doing something right. I wanted to always be honest with Lennon about my motives, and to show her that while I loved her, I could also be independent and go after things that I wanted.

So I decided to buzz him up. "Mom, can you just hit the button for the lobby door?"

I heard her hit it while I put the earring in my lobe, and then I headed for the living room.

"Well, it's just a party in here, isn't it?" Jake smirked as I opened the door, Lennon belting "Be Our Guest" behind me in her underwear.

He leaned in for a hug, the scent of sandalwood cologne surrounding me. I could feel the bulge of his arms through the rolled up sleeves of his button up, and I wanted to stay like this for a long time. If only my mother wasn't waiting for us, probably cataloging the amount of seconds we hugged.

"Sorry for the chaos, but I thought it would be good for her to know where I was going. Or she'll ask a million questions. Hell, she'll ask a million questions anyway."

"It's a good thing I brought this then." He pulled out one of those big rainbow lollipops, and followed it with a small bouquet of flowers. "Lennon, this is for you."

She turned, stopping her theatrical performance, and ran with little grabby hands to him. "Ohhhhh! Tank you!"

Jake bent down to give it to her, my view of his perfectly sculpted ass just a plus as he interacted with my daughter.

"And these, Molly, are for you. Beautiful flowers for a beautiful woman."

Okay, now he was just being a kiss ass. And my mother fell right for his trap.

"Oh Jake, how sweet of you! And sunflowers, my favorite." She batted her eyelashes at him like she was some kind of cartoon princess.

"Yuck, enough. Is this your way of trying to get me to like you? Ignore the girl you're interested in while giving attention to the ones you're not?" I rolled my eyes in a dramatic way, teasing him.

He leaned in for only us to hear. "You get the big present later, if you know what I mean.

It was cheesy as hell, but my lady parts still perked up at the titillating innuendo.

"So, you ready to go? You look gorgeous by the way." He stuck out his arm like he was about to escort me to the elevators.

"I told her so!" Mom chimed in, still trying to get Jake's attention.

"Yeah, I am, just let me grab my purse. Lennon, come give Mommy a kiss goodbye."

She didn't budge from in front of the TV, and I knew she wouldn't for the next half an hour. Walking to her, I bent down and smacked a wet one on her cheek.

"Ick, Mommy, messy! Bring home ice cream?" She stuck her chubby little hand in her mouth, and I didn't know when she'd be able to disassociate Jake with ice cream.

Probably never. Which probably meant his business plan was working well.

"All right, I'll be home soon," I said, turning to my mother.

"I'll make sure to have her home by eleven, and don't worry, we won't go parking or anything." Jake winked at my mom.

I had to roll my eyes again as she giggled while we were walking out the door.

"You're quite the charmer, you know. It's probably what makes you such a good business owner." I pointed my fork at him over the best seafood gnocchi I'd ever eaten in my life.

"It's a gift and a curse. Women, they just flock to me." Jake folds his hands, very talented hands might I add, under his chin like a good Catholic school boy.

"I'll overlook that cocky comment if you'll give me another bite of that pork risotto." I stuck my fork across the table, nabbing a mouthful of his delicious plate.

"You know what I learned about you on this date? You're a fork vulture. You're one of those people who takes bites off another person's plate without asking."

I chuckle self-consciously. "And that's a bad thing? We're on a date, isn't it assumed that I get to taste your meal too?"

"Actually, it's kind of cute. And I don't mind at all. This place is one of my favorites, so I'm glad you like it." His green eyes flicker with the dance of the candle in between us.

"Like it? I think I'm going to move in over there by the kitchen and let them feed me as a form of rent."

I wasn't joking. Every course had been better than the last. And with a self-proclaimed wine expert, in all honesty he really did know his stuff, the drinks were paired fabulously. All in all, it had been a really great date ... one that I surprisingly did not want to end. I felt the minutes ticking by, like I was Cinderella at the ball and at midnight I'd turn into a pumpkin whose daughter climbed into bed with her in the middle of the night and kicked her in the face.

"So, I know we've had some great conversation, but now I'm going to ask the dreaded 'first couple of dates' questions because I need to get to know you a little deeper if I'm going to allow you to take me out for a second fantastic meal." I folded my napkin in my lap, squaring with him.

He fake shuddered. "Oh God, just rip the bandage off quick, gorgeous."

I didn't want to make things awkward, but we'd spent two dates and a hot night of sex together, and it was time to go below the surface. I knew he was funny, charming and handsome. I knew about his business, and that he could give just as good as he got in conversation ... and in other areas that concerned men and women. But we hadn't really gotten all that personal, and if I was really going to dive head first into the dating pool with someone again, I needed to know if the water was nice.

"Jake Brady, when was your last relationship?"

15

JAKE

I knew that it would get to this point. At some time or another, every relationship did.

With some women, it happened two hours into the first meeting ... in which case I was running in the opposite direction. No two people needed to exchange life stories over the first cup of coffee or beer they ever ordered together.

And apparently, with Samantha, the time was now. It didn't mean I wanted to get into all the personal stuff, who ever wanted to relive their fuck ups and sordid past, but for her ... I'd make the exception. I don't know if I'd ever been so ready to be forthcoming with a woman before.

I sighed, twining my fingers with hers as I started. "If we're going to go there, I'm allowed to touch you. My last *relationship*, if you could call it that, was about six months ago. She was a local graduate student, we dated for a couple of months, nothing serious. She was too young, and I was too uninterested. It might not be what you want to hear, but there is the truth."

I hesitate to look up, not wanting to see her reaction.

"Jake, look at me." Her soft voice sounded from across the table, and I met her dark eyes. "I'm not doing this to shame you or get dirt, I just want to know where you've been. What your life has looked like, because I want to know you. Thank you for being honest with me."

Nodding, I kind of saw her point. "Well then, since you want my past, it's not a very storied one. I've dated ... a lot, but nothing serious. A few months here or there, no next steps, nothing that ever made me want to pursue it into another level. I've focused on my business a lot, and just kind of went about life with the flow that I always have. It might sound stupid, but you're really the first woman I've felt a real connection with, and I'm not just saying that because I've seen you naked. Although ... goddamn, that was a fun experience. Samantha, I don't know what to say ... I just, there is something here. So there is the truth. I have no skeletons, sure I've probably been a jerk and dumped my fair share of wonderful women because I was an idiot, but I've never cheated. I've never been engaged or lived with a woman. I've slept with women, and that's as far as I'll go. But, I'm an open book. Because I like you. So if there is anything you'd ever like to know, just ask."

I think a fly went into her mouth with how far down it was hanging. "How do you manage to do that? Take my expectations and blow them right out of the water?

"I get it right about seventy percent of the time. Don't forget the zoo ... that started off well until I crashed and burned."

She smirked, squeezing my hand. "To be fair, Lennon did have quite the meltdown."

I toyed with the napkin in my lap, trying to figure out how to ask my next question. "So now that you know about me ... can you tell me a little bit about your past relationships?"

Her face contorts from one of teasing happiness to a far-away, masked loneliness. I know it won't be easy, but we have to talk about it, like she said. I need to know what *I'm* getting into ... because as I'd said, I did care about her. I was interested in pursuing this, much further than I'd ever thought about pursing anything with any other woman.

"It's really only one relationship. Sure, I dated in the flirty, kind of teenage way before I met my ex, but before him it was nothing real. I met Derek when I was nineteen, at Madison in our sophomore year. He was ... my first love. I loved him completely. After we graduated, I had no idea what I wanted to do, so when he was offered a job out in Seattle, I went with him. More like followed him, I guess. After we got out there, our relationship changed, even if I didn't want to admit it to myself. I'm not sure what happened, but he just wasn't ... present, I guess. I hung in there, thinking that if we could only make it to him proposing, to a wedding, to *something*, then it would all be all right."

A sad smile crosses her face, and I can feel the pain in her voice. I can see how ignored she felt, and I instantly want to slam my fist into this Derek guy's jaw.

"I found my job at Mount Rainier and fell in love, so Seattle did give me something. Two things, actually. Two years into living out there, I got pregnant with Lennon. It was a massive surprise, but for a little at least, it seemed to bring Derek and I back together. He was supportive and excited, and I thought it was finally the thing that would make us a family. Except six months after she was born, as I was trying to juggle being a new mother and holding down a job and not going insane, he just checked out. Started talking about traveling to foreign countries, and spreading his wings. I really tried to make us work, it absolutely kills me that Lennon will have to grow up with two parents who were never married and are no longer together. But by her third birthday, I just couldn't do it anymore. I couldn't sit in that house every night with a complete stranger. We didn't love each other anymore, and I was doing more harm to my daughter staying with him. So I left."

She shrugs, and it looks like she's trying to shrug the heaviness of everything she'd been through off of her shoulders. Sadness comes off of her in waves, but there is something else there too. Relief? Freedom? Something resembling the two.

I take her hand, the one woven in mine, in my other hand, encasing it. "You made a really tough decision, but one that was better in the long run for you and Lennon. Thank you for telling me that ... I know it wasn't easy. Any man who doesn't give you all of the love and attention you deserve, both you and Lennon, doesn't deserve you. I've seen how you are with that little girl, and any man ..."

I have to break off, because I feel myself getting angry. She's not even my kid, hell I haven't even spent that much time with her, but I saw how awesome she is. I have never understood how someone could bring a child into this world and not be completely enthralled with everything they did.

"Anyway, now that we got that off our plate, literally ... what's for dessert?" She smiled, her expression breaking up the invisible cobwebs of the past on her face.

She needed me to transition us. So I did. "And now we come to the most important part of the date, because it will determine the probability of me asking you out again ... are you a chocolate cake or cheesecake kind of person?"

Samantha contemplated me for a second, our hands still holding on to the other. "You're asking me out no matter what, let's face it. But I'll go with the cheesecake."

I winked, loving her confidence. "A girl who knows what she wants and can order the right thing too, I knew I picked well."

We finished up our dessert and then walked to the car, the night balmy. It was one of those perfect summer nights, one where I would have liked to take her to the steps of the Lincoln Memorial to sit and watch the lights of the city. But I knew she had to get home, and the date had already been so damn near perfect I didn't want to ruin it.

I drove her home, taking the time to get out of the car and follow her into the building.

"You don't have to come up, it's okay. You know you can't come in ..." She looks so beautiful as she timidly tries to let me down.

As much as I'd like to lift the skirt of her hot-as-fuck dress up and plunge into her in the middle of this lobby, I know why I can't stay with her tonight.

"I'm a gentleman bringing you up to your front door, can't I do that?" My motives were so not that pure, but I didn't want to walk away just yet.

"Okay." She wove her fingers through mine as we walked to the elevator.

We rode up in silence, our hands the only things connecting us. How badly did I want to push her up against the wall? So fucking badly that I had to bite my tongue to remain a good boy.

As we arrived on her floor, Samantha took her keys out of her purse and led me out, walking to her door just a few short steps from the elevator.

"Thank you for a really great date." She turned to me, her chocolate eyes smiling contently.

I didn't respond. Instead, I gently pushed her up against the wall, taking both sides of her face in my hands before I laid my lips on hers. I'd waited all fucking week to kiss her, to taste her, to feel her ... and I was taking full advantage of this moment.

She had the most kissable mouth, soft and full with just a little bit of fight. I explored her lips lazily, tangling our tongues and plunging mine in deep, almost slowly fucking her mouth with my own. A small moan worked its way up her throat and into mine, and a sizzle of electricity held me by the balls. My fingers felt the smooth skin beneath them, itching to move south.

I broke off the deep, intimate connection and placed a kiss on the tip of her nose before moving away. I didn't trust myself not to try and get her naked in the middle of this hallway.

"Good night, Samantha. I'll call you tomorrow."

She still stood there as I backed away, a little dazed as she watched me get back in the elevator.

Hell yeah, it was a *really* great date.

16

JAKE

Dozens of trucks lined the waterfront, the fairgrounds teeming with people. This was my Graceland, my Woodstock.

Truckapalooza was the one event of the year where we did our most business, outselling ourselves and usually depleting our stock. It was a chance to get the Cones & Corks name out there, and to make impressions on industry bigwigs who secretly combed the scene, looking for the next big foodie obsession.

"Oh my God, you have got to try this truffle mac n'cheese." Alice practically moans as she shoves another forkful in her mouth.

I set down the heavy container of green tea ice cream I'm carrying and stare at her. "Are you fucking kidding me? Focus, please. We have ten more minutes to stock and then we'll be slammed the rest of the day."

"Yes, boss man." She salutes me, a piece of her now cotton-candy pink hair flying up. "You know I work better on a full stomach, though. Don't worry, I'm going to charm the pants and wallets right off those investors."

If I wasn't so sure of that statement myself, I would be more jittery. But she was good, we both knew it. And I had high hopes for today.

"Maybe we'll get a storefront. Or *hey*! Maybe, Target will want to pick us up and put us in those little cafes in the front of their stores. God, I love Target. You wouldn't think I would, but just something about all of the shit you could ever want being in the same location."

I had to laugh at her zeal, but wasn't trying to dream too big. It had been three years since the business had been born, and we were doing great. But I wanted more, and as the owner, I had to put my neck on the guillotine time and time again to get it. They, whoever *they* were, weren't kidding when they said running your own business was damn tough.

"Who would have figured you for a Target junkie?" We began sliding the front windows to the truck open and setting up our promotional materials on the counters outside.

"It's actually a great date spot. See the weird things that people pick out, whether they match up with your weird things. This one time, a chick picked out a shaving kit, a pair of high-heeled sandals, and some weed killer. I couldn't get past how odd the combination was ... it made me like her even more. You should try it sometime with your little single mommy."

A boom of laughter erupted from my throat, because I could definitely see Alice taking a date to Target just to get under their skin. "Her name is Samantha, you know that. And retract the claws when she comes around today, she's bringing her daughter."

She holds her hands up as if to say, "who me?"

"You're just worried I might steal her away. You know, since I'm better in bed than you are."

I roll my eyes, setting out the last of our supplies before the truck is throttled with customers. "Not everyone is interested in a lesbian experience with you."

"Pshh, how would you know? My hips don't lie and neither do the abilities of my tongue."

It's the last dirty remark she makes for a while, as the food truck fair gets going and the grounds become even more crowded. We both scoop and pour as we network, getting people to follow us on social media, post pictures, take brochures. I just recently opened an option on the website for catering, and a bunch of engaged couples throughout the day express their interest in our truck being the favors at their weddings. It's exciting and I can feel the adrenaline buzzing through my veins with every sale and sample I hand out.

"I don't even get to cut the line and I'm dating the proprietor."

I swing back to the window just in time to see Samantha, Lennon and Molly walk up.

"Will a kiss do instead?" I lean out the window, checking out cleavage as I stare down on her.

In the week since our date, I hadn't seen her. Sure, we'd talked on the phone, and even had some phone sex after Lennon had gone to bed, but it wasn't easy dating a woman who had priorities that came before a relationship. I was trying to be patient, and I understood, but fuck was it hard not to see her whenever I wanted.

"Only if it comes with a side of whatever Midnight Caramel Cow is ... because that sounds amazing." She scans the side of the truck, with our signature flavors of the day written on it.

"Come around back." I nod to the door and walk to meet her on the other side.

As soon as I make it outside, she's there, a yellow and blue sundress molding to her curves.

"Good to see you." I tip her chin up with my hand, kissing her out of sight of the chaos in the front of the truck.

"Where the heck is my sample? I wasn't coming back here to fool around, I really wanted ice cream."

"I'll give you some cream." I wink, knowing my dimple has popped out.

She shoves my arm half-heartedly. "Gross."

"What else did you eat so far?"

"Oh, just about a bite of everything. This is insane, but I will report that I've heard great things being said about this truck right here all afternoon. You're definitely one of the more buzzed about businesses, just so you know."

Her news made my chest puff out a little. "Your spy skills may have just bought you a free cone."

The back door to the truck swings open, and Alice climbs down the steps, a weird look on her face. She approaches Samantha and I, her black army boots completely standing out in the summer heat.

"So, you're the MILF, huh? I get it now." She nods at Samantha like she's assessing her as a piece of livestock for sale at a show.

"All right, that's enough. I told you, no claws, please." I had to roll my eyes and shake my head at Samantha, Jim Halpert-style.

I knew Alice could be blunt, but she was practically sniffing my girl and trying to pee on me at the same time.

"What, I'm just complimenting her. She's hot. And if she's anywhere near as cool as you say she is, he talks about you a shit ton, then I'm happy for you, man."

She pats me on the back and walks back up the truck steps, out to the masses.

"Jesus, sorry about that. She's a little ... direct."

Samantha wraps her arms around my waist, her small frame fitting perfectly in mine. I don't know when we went from touching each other only at certain moments in private, to showing affection in public, but I liked it. Normally, it wouldn't be my favorite thing a girl could do. But I noticed that every time Samantha took our what was happening between us just a touch further, I wanted to take it a mile longer.

"I actually kind of like her. And she called me a MILF, so she's good in my book."

I bent down, kissing her neck and allowing her smell to wash over me. "That's because you are a mother I'd like to fuck. A mother I do fuck, a very sexy woman who makes the sweetest moans when I suck on her—"

"Ooookay, horn dog, you're going to make me mount you in a public park. And then we'd both be arrested for public indecency. Is that what you want?" She put her hands on my chest.

"Would you believe me if I said I didn't care in this moment?"

The wind blew some of her silky dark strands in her face as she laughed. "Yes. But you have to work, and I need some ice cream. So get to it."

Her hand landed squarely on my khaki-clad ass cheek, giving it a firm pat.

"Did you just spank me, sweetheart?" I was probably sporting a semi on her thigh now.

"Maybe ..."

"Go get your Mom and Lennon, you three come on into the truck. You can help us serve, and eat all the ice cream you want. Do it now before I drag you to that porta potty over there."

Her eyes twinkled with laughter and arousal as she skipped away. Damn, I was really infatuated with this woman.

The rest of the afternoon was spent in the crowded truck, which I usually despised if more than two people were working in it. But today, with all three Groff girls chirping around the small metal canister, it was actually kind of fun. Molly was a natural with customers, and Samantha was a little bossy pants who kept things organized. Lennon mostly just ate ice cream, but for a while she chatted with customers and drew people to the truck. I knew it was a plus to have a cute kid around sometimes.

All in all, it was one of the best days I'd ever spent working on my business. And I knew it was not a coincidence that the new lady in my life was there for it.

17

"No, no, put me on the phone with them. *NOW.*" I tried not to scream, but it had been that kind of day.

The fire marshal got on the phone, explaining the situation, as my rangers in California squawked in the background. My head hurt, my vision was getting fuzzy, and it was way past the time that I was supposed to be at work.

After a few more instructions and handing out my cell phone number to a bunch of various sources, I hung up, letting my forehead hit the desk. I probably had another hour here of emails and reports, and I was so drained I felt worse than the time I'd been in labor for sixteen hours. Just kidding ... but in this moment, it felt close.

The forest fire in one of our California national parks had started three days ago, but it had reached peak temperatures and ravaging today. I'd been on the phone all day, trying to calm people down, trying to formulate a plan, get answers.

My cell phone rings on the desk, my lamp the only thing illuminating the office now. Everyone had headed home, but I couldn't in good conscience, go.

"Hello?" I snap into the speaker, not bothering to see who it is.

"Hey sweetie ... I know you're busy today, but remember I have that poker night with the girls?" Mom's voice was tentative and sweet, and I knew she wasn't trying to get me riled up.

Shit, I hadn't remembered. And Lennon was still at her house. And I had to be here for the foreseeable hours. Typically, I never complained about being a mother. Sure, there were the little everyday gripes, but I knew how lucky I was with my daughter, and how lucky I was to have a mother nearby now who provided so much help.

But it was times like right now that my internal struggle was the worst. That my need to feel like a good mother, and also a successful employee, was completely conflicting.

It didn't help that Derek had texted me today, cancelling his plans to come out here yet again. It had been two and a half months since we'd moved here, and in that time, he hadn't bothered to come visit his daughter once. I was past annoyance and onto the stage of indifference, which was probably worse. If he didn't care about being in her life, than I wouldn't concern myself with it either.

"I'm sorry, Mom, it's been a hard day. I'll ... I'll be there soon." That was a lie, and I knew that I would be sacrificing one or the other.

And even though it was something that made me tear up, that thing was usually my career.

I dropped my head into my hands, massaging my throbbing temples as I tried to formulate a plan and stand up from my desk.

My cell phone rings again, and I'm reluctant to even look at it as I know my mother is probably badgering me about her social outing tonight.

"Yes, Mom, I'll be right there."

"Oh hey, did I get you at a bad time?"

Jake's voice filters through my ear, a more soothing dose of medicine than I knew it could be. I choke up, my anxiety and rationality strings almost completely cut.

"Sorry, it's been a ... rough day. I thought you were my mom, I have to pick Lennon up but I also need to work—"

"You're still at work?"

I looked at the clock which read seven p.m. "That I am. There have been a bunch of brush fires that turned into forest fires today in California, and I've been dealing with crisis all day. Now I have to drive over to pick her up, but should be stapled to my desk ..."

I felt my nerves fraying.

"I don't want to overstep but ... let me pick her up. I'll grab your keys from your mom and take Lennon home so you can work."

My immediate reaction was no. "That's okay, I'll figure something else out."

I didn't want to tell him that I was still unsure about really introducing him into Lennon's life. As of now, he'd just been a ... *friend* that we saw on the weekends sometimes. One that mommy talked to on the phone, or who dropped by with a treat now and then.

"Come on, Samantha, I want to help. You can trust her with me, I want to be there for you in any way I can. And you need to work."

The idea toyed in my brain, two sides completely at war. Was it too soon for him to become integral to her? What would happen if we broke up? But what would happen if this was really great, for both myself and my daughter? Was I scared of that?

Yes. I was a wimp. History had shown me that men didn't stick around for my daughter.

"I know it's a big step for you, it's a step for me too. But it's one I want to take. So please, let me pick Lennon up." His voice was quiet but serious, and I knew that he knew the weight of this too.

Hesitantly, I pushed aside the fear and pulled up my big girl panties. "Oh ... okay. Full disclosure? I'm not one hundred percent on board, but I know that you would never let anything happen to my daughter. That she is my life and if you ever harmed a hair on her head, I'd hunt you down and cut off your balls."

"Duly noted. I will drive the speed limit, not feed her candy, fight off any rabid dogs, not become a victim to the bedtime story beg ... anything else?"

His sarcasm was putting me a little more at ease, but I took on my tough mom tone. "My mom will give you the spare key she has, and I'll call her and my doorman to let them know you're approved to take care of Lennon. She's already had dinner most likely, so if she wants she can have one cookie or a pack of fruit snacks before bed. Don't worry about bath time, and she'll know how to get into her pajamas herself so just leave her to that. She likes a sippy-cup of water on the nightstand, preferably her Nemo cup, and only read her one bedtime story. Because as you said, it'll be like waterboard torture if you don't stop at one. You'll be reading until your eyes fall out."

Silence met me at the other end of the phone. "Jake?"

He cleared his throat. "Sorry, I was just typing it all down in an email to myself so I make sure I won't forget anything. I'll text you when I pick her up, when we get to the apartment, and when she goes to sleep."

My heart sped up a beat, a tickle forming in my throat. "Thank you for doing this. You don't know how much it means. I'll try to wrap up here soon."

"You don't have to thank me, Samantha, I want to be a

support system for you. Just take your time, I know how important this is for those people out in California."

His willingness to take care of Lennon was sexier than
anything he'd done thus far, and he couldn't possibly know how
much he'd just melted another large chunk of the iceberg that
had become my heart since the breakup.

We hung up, my stress level going down marginally, but my
anxiety tethering to what was happening with Jake and Lennon.
I got back to work, waiting for his texts to come through.

18

Backing away from the door, I closed it so gingerly that you'd think there was a bomb about to explode instead of an adorable three-year-old girl.

No one ever told me that dealing with a toddler was like deciding whether to cut the red wire or the blue wire. If I put in a Disney movie, depending on which one, would she get more tired and settle down or would it amp her up? Would an Oreo give her a sugar high, or were strawberry fruit snacks the way to go? When she asked for a bedtime story, which one put her to sleep and which had her pleading for another story?

I was literally more exhausted than I'd ever been in my life, tiredness seeped into the marrow of my bones, and I had no idea how Samantha did this every day. If anything, it made me want to kiss her entire body in worship. If I was able to get up off this couch without my muscles protesting.

It had taken me two hours to accomplish everything that I knew Samantha would have done in about half an hour. I picked Lennon up, answered her fifty questions in the car, got her into the apartment while juggling bags of her things, chased her around trying to get her changed and settled, and then finagled with her to finally fall asleep.

I'd just run a marathon, and I felt my eyes drooping as the apartment locks squeaked.

"Hello ..." Samantha walked in, her thighs rubbing against the long pencil skirt she wore.

Damn, this was a sight I could get used to coming home to.

"Shhh! Be very, very quiet. There is a child hunting adults," I whispered in my best Elmer Fudd accent.

"Well, I can see who won this battle." Her smile is tired but happy, and I want to wrap my hands around her shoulders and squeeze.

Hearing her sigh while I massage her ... yeah, that's what I want right fucking now.

"Hey, I got her to sleep, didn't I? I'd say I slayed the giant." I patted myself on the back. Literally.

She set her oversized purse down—what did women carry in there anyway?—and came to sit next to me on the couch.

"Thank you for taking care of her tonight, Jake. Seriously, it's above and beyond what should be asked of you, and I really appreciate it."

She leans forward and lightly kisses me, an action I can feel tugging at my balls. It's a miracle I can think straight around this woman.

"Why do you keep doing that?" I can't help but be a little bit offended, and I move back on the couch.

It's a total passive aggressive, looking for a fight move, and I know it. I feel like a wimp, but I don't like that she discounts me like that.

Samantha sighs, taking her hair out of the clip it was in so that it pools around her shoulders. Momentarily, I'm distracted, because Jesus she is radiant. Even after a tough day at work, she looks like she just stepped off the pages of a Maxim magazine

... kind of like the ones I'd hide under my bed when I was fifteen.

"Jake, you said at the beginning that you wanted to take this slow, that you weren't looking to become a father. I guess I've just been trying to respect that."

"Well, what if I changed my mind?" I know I sound like the three-year-old now.

"You don't get to change your mind when it comes to a child. You have to be all in, even on the worst days." Her smile is sympathetic.

I muster up all of my gusto. "I'm here for everything, I want you to know that. I may have said those things in the beginning, but we have gone slow. A date night here, a week of talking and not seeing each other. A couple of hours with Lennon. And do you know what I feel in those moments when I'm not here with you two? I miss you. I miss this. I may not understand the full extent of it, but I haven't been given the chance to be here for the three years you've had with her. I'm allowed to be a little unsure, as I'm sure you are some days too. I do know that I want more, that we should give this a real try. That I want you to count on me, not just come to me in crisis. I'm in this, with you. With her. Give me that chance."

There is a long pause, the light from the TV changing on our faces as cartoon characters dance across the screen. Samantha's expression is unreadable, and my heart pounds so much that I'm scared I'll actually throw the organ up.

"So what, do you want to be my boyfriend, then?" She rolls her eyes, settling back into my arms and ghosting her lips over my neck.

"As a thirty-year-old bachelor, am I too old to be a boyfriend?" I tease her, sliding my hand up under the material of her shirt.

"Hm, I don't think so. As long as you don't think that having a twenty-seven-year-old girlfriend is robbing the cradle."

It was childish, and almost surreal, that my heart jumped when she said the word girlfriend.

I rubbed my hand up and down her back in comforting circles. "I mean, I would also take King of Your Heart, Master of Your Soul, Fetcher of Your Purse. Doesn't really matter to me, so you settle on which one is best."

Samantha lets out a low chuckle, one that has me hardening in my pants instantly. "All the above. But just so we're clear ... we're really doing this? The monogamy thing? Because I don't take that lightly. You know my past, you know that I want more than just a warm body next to me."

I stare straight into her eyes, trying to relay my message to the deepest part of her. "I know what you need, and I want to give it to you."

For a second, we just sit on the couch in the silence, the weight of commitment passing between us.

She breaks it, rubbing my leg over my pants. "And since you want to give me that, I want to give you something too."

I smile and I can see her eye my dimple.

"Oh don't get so ahead of yourself, King of my Heart. It's late, and I want you to stay here if you want to. But you also can't stay in bed with me ... confusion for the kid and all. So to celebrate our first night of monogamy, I invite you to sleep on my couch."

Her words carried sarcasm, but there was worry mixed in her tone as well. I knew how much this meant, what the stakes were for Samantha. She was letting me in, even if it was a foot halfway into the hallway and not all the way into the proverbial bedroom. It'll be torture to sleep just feet from her, but she's giving me a chance, the very thing I asked for.

If I can do this, sleep on her too-small couch overnight, then we'll wake up in a very different place. For one, I'll get to make her eggs again. But Samantha will also have to begin to explain and introduce Lennon to the idea of me ... and that's a giant leap for Jake-kind.

"Do I at least get a pillow and a blanket? And maybe a good night blow job?" Gently, I push her back.

My lips meet her neck, sucking and tasting the sweet skin beneath her ear. My hands find her ribs, touch the edges of her lace bra.

"Jake ..." She groans, arousal and scolding mixing together in her voice.

"I know, gorgeous, but I'm just showing you what you'll be missing while you're lying in that big, empty bed without me." I was being a taunting prick, but she felt too damn good.

Samantha slides out from under me like a ninja, leaving me *very* high and very dry.

"And you'll be out here, sleeping with Lennon's Dora the Explorer blanket. So don't be a dirty dog, because Boots sees everything."

She whispers in my ear before sashaying away, giving me a very nice view. Just when a guy gets a girlfriend, he gets completely cock-blocked.

And honestly, the night squished on the couch in the living room was one of the best in a while.

19

JAKE

I straightened the pencil cup on my desk one more time, looking around to make sure everything was in place.

"You look like a schizo right now ..." Alice slings her bag over her shoulder.

"Stop it! He looks cute. He's just trying to impress his girlfriend, give him some much deserved credit. I never thought I'd see the day honestly."

"You ladies do know that I'm right here, right?" I looked up, amused, as Alice and Jana stand in the doorway of my office.

"Whoops, I knew we should have learned Morse code, like Jim and Pam did on *The Office*. We could talk about him so much more easily in his presence." Alice scratches her nose with her middle finger.

It's the end of the day at the end of a long week. After the food truck festival, there has been some buzz about Cones & Corks ... the exact kind of buzz we were aiming for. Alice has already met with two potential investors who are interested in bringing us to a storefront. I couldn't be any more psyched about it, or fucking nervous. Deals like this took time, and often fell through. Even if we did sign a contract, there was no guarantee that a commercial location would be successful. There was so much up in the air that I felt as if I were juggling six plates that were also lit on fire.

But I had no time for worry tonight. Well, except when it came to impressing my girlfriend. Samantha was on her way over to see our offices, and I wanted everything to be perfect. Mostly because this would be our first couple of hours alone in a week; I'd slept on the couch again two nights ago since things went well the first time. I'd woken up to Lennon almost drawing on my face in Sharpie marker before Samantha screamed at her ... what a beautiful way to open your eyes to the world.

"Go home, you deserve it." As much as I wanted to eventually introduce my friends to Samantha, I wanted her all to myself tonight.

"We get it, we're going. Just don't have sex on my desk." Jana wags her finger at me.

Alice bursts out laughing as she walks toward the front door. "She said it, not me."

They leave in a fit of laughter, and I should yell back something sarcastic, but my phone vibrates on the desk.

Samantha: *I'll be there in two.*

Jake: *I'll be the one with no pants on.*

I was only semi-kidding. Because ever since she'd agreed to come have a tour of the office, I'd been thinking about fucking her brains out on my desk.

Walking out to the front door, I waited to see car lights come around the corner and into the parking lot. The sun was setting, the nights getting darker more quickly as the end of August approached. The sky was streaked with pink and purple, the clouds looking to blend in like marshmallows. Soon it would be fall, and then winter. We'd go into hibernation, because who the hell ran out to the sidewalk for the ice cream truck in three feet of snow? That's why I was banking on this storefront. Not that it would be ready until next year, but I could just imagine coming up with creative cold month flavors. Eggnog, pumpkin spice, cranberry mulled wine ... the thought had me wanting to go into the test kitchen and whip some up right now.

Headlights shine in my eyes, and then Samantha is swinging her car into a spot.

"Hi, you." Her smile is my undoing as she gets out.

Long legs in a white work skirt stride toward me, and I may have to swallow my tongue to keep it from lolling on the ground like one of those cartoon characters. Post-work Samantha may be my favorite look of hers. She's like a sexy librarian fantasy, and I'm the student who needs a tutor.

"Hi back, baby." The skin on her arms is pure velvet under my fingers, and when I kiss her, it's like a nice long sip of Merlot after a long day.

"So, show me the digs. I want to see where the magic happens."

Lacing my fingers in hers, I lead her inside. "You've already been in my bedroom."

"Har, har, he's got jokes. Seriously, I'm only here for the ice cream so you better step to it."

I show her the boring office side of the building first, explaining where everyone sits. I'm tempted to relive my fantasy on my desk, but know that the more exciting part of the tour is in the test kitchen and machine room.

Samantha asks questions about how we really got started, what the early days were like, and how we all take chunks of the business now. It boosts my ego to have someone I care about take an interest in what I do, because I'm not really used to this. No one in my life besides my coworkers and possibly Bryan give a shit about what I do ... they'd rather have me hocking SUVs and four-wheel drive all day.

"And this ... this is my Bat Cave." I wave my hand around the test kitchen, all of the gleaming machines and counters greeting us like star pupils.

"I get it, since you drive an ice cream shaped car. Not as flashy as the classic black mobile, but it'll do." She walks around the room, inspecting all of the machines.

"Sometimes I sit in here until the early hours of the morning, just creating new recipes. Some of them are absolutely terrible." I can't help but chuckle, thinking about the salted peanut butter and jelly flavor I'd whipped up.

One would think it would be delicious, but it was so salty, it might as well have been straight out of the Atlantic ocean.

"You're like an evil genius in his laboratory ... except, you know, with sugar and cream." Samantha walks to me, running her hands up my arms.

Being alone with her, in the silence, after so many hours waiting for it ... I kind of don't know what to do. I feel like a teenage boy trying to decide how to make the next move on a girl.

"So, let me do some taste testing. That's the real reason I came here."

Moving to the industrial freezer nestled between the granite counters on one wall, I take three containers out of it. I grab a scoop and two spoons, no bowls.

Samantha hops up onto the counter, her skirt riding up her thighs just a couple of inches. Enough to make me want more, but not enough to give me a full view of her. We haven't had sex since the one time at my apartment, although I've wanted to so badly that my cock physically hurts when I'm around her. It's amazing how little time one has for themselves when a child is involved.

"Okay, first one is a bourbon s'mores flavor." I scoop a little spoonful and hold it out to her.

Her lips close around it, pulling the ice cream off the utensil, and I imagine her doing that to a part of my anatomy. I watch as her face relaxes and blisses out, and that right there is always the reaction I'm looking for. I crave it on my customer's faces, but I find that with Samantha, it's also an aphrodisiac. Watching her enjoy what I've made turns me on like a lightbulb.

"Mmm, give me another." Her eyebrow raises and I know this is a sexy game for her just as much as it is for me.

Moving to the next quart, I scoop her a little bigger of a spoonful of pistachio white chocolate. "This one is non-alcoholic, but I think you'll like it."

She darts her tongue out preemptively, the motion making it hard for me to take my eyes from her mouth. And because of that, I don't see the two drips that fall onto her leg, just below her knee and narrowly missing her skirt.

"Oops ..." She looks down, but then back up and quickly swipes a lick of the flavor off the spoon. "Totally worth the mess, that is delicious."

"I think I like you messy, means I can clean up."

The air in the room shifts, arousal and heat swamping the space between us.

I bend at the waist, my eyes never leaving hers. With that gaze I told her exactly what I was going to do, and I could see those chocolate pools melt under the notion that I was about to devour her. My hands grip the bare parts of her thighs, squeezing gently to let her know what's coming.

Picking up one toned, smooth leg, I lower my mouth to where the ice cream dripped. And lick it off her skin, all the way up as my hands move her skirt higher.

This was my test kitchen, and Samantha just happened to be the best flavor I'd ever tasted.

"That's one great batch." I lick my lip where a bit of the ice cream remains.

She's scooted back on the counter now, her hands pressed

against the gleaming tops and her legs spread a little wider. Her cheeks are flushed and her hair is tossed over both shoulders, her head hanging slightly back. Slowly, she picks up a hand. Dips a finger into the s'mores flavor. And rubs the chocolate ice cream over her collar bone.

"I think you dropped some here, too." The gleam in her eyes is pure devilish.

I walk into her body, getting as close as the counter will allow me and then moving her the rest of the way until I'm positioned perfectly between her thighs. My cock lengthens, the hardness becoming uncomfortable against the closed zipper of my pants. My mouth seeks her skin, licking lightly at her collarbone. Samantha's scent and the ice cream mix, making my head spin. I don't ever think I've nearly buckled at the knees from a woman, but this one just made me swoon.

"You taste delicious. I may have to add you to the menu ..." I keep sucking on her neck, loving the way it makes her grind harder against me.

"But only for Jake Brady, party of one." She giggles on a moan as I push her skirt farther up.

My hands reach lace, and my cock begs again to be set free. Something about the thin material of her panties under my fingertips sets me off, and I can't play this slow, teasing game much longer.

"I should be slow, take my time ... but it's been almost a month since I've been inside of you and I can't play the gentleman ..." My voice is hoarse.

"So don't. Please, God, don't." She shimmies herself on the counter, pulling her underwear free and throwing it to the ground.

Samantha's face is focused on my hands as they undo my jeans and pull down the zipper. Her shirt is askew, a button or two undone from where I'd kissed and licked her. Her skirt is hiked up around her waist, that pretty pussy gleaming at me.

Releasing myself, we both gasp. Me from the bittersweet pain of the cool air on my erection, and her from watching as I make my way towards her.

"I don't have a condom ..." My steps stutter.

"I'm on the pill. Hurry ..." She licks her lips, her expression wild.

Arousal wraps its fierce hands around my spine, sending shockwaves straight to my balls. I have to bite my tongue from going buck wild, because I need to at least make this last long enough so that she comes first. But being raw inside of her ... Jesus, I may just up and die right here on the spot.

Hands fist in my hair as I grip her hips, her legs molding around me and locking as they pull my ass in. My jeans hang somewhere between my thighs and knees, our clothes completely askew and in the way. But there is no time, I need her too much.

"Fuck ..." I hiss as I push into her, the sweet zing of being inside of her with no barrier comparing to nothing else I've ever felt.

Samantha's head drops back, a low moan escaping her lips. I pump my hips, testing the tight slide of her. My cock twitches and my hands shake where they hold her, fury about to unleash from every cell in my body.

"I'm not going to be gentle." I bite out the words.

"Please, Jake, for God's sake, give it to me."

Her forehead presses to mine and then we're off, all of the pent up sexual frustration that has existed between us for a month being let out. All of the weeks of texting, the nights on the couch, the first awful date and the slow build up afterward ... it all comes crashing down as I pump into her frantically.

We're shoving each other's clothes up and aside, her hands

fist under my shirt, nails raking across the hair on my chest. One of mine tangles in her hair, pulling it back to expose her neck so I can feast. My other fingers find her right nipple, pushing the cup of her bra down so it pushes her breast up.

There is no skilled rhythm here, no slow exploration. We're racing to the finish line of our climaxes, and I'm going dumb, deaf and blind from the amount of pleasure rocketing through my system.

"OH GOD!" Samantha lets out a cry, her voice loud and ringing through the empty building.

She pulses around me and I lose it, the explosion of total gratification numbing my brain to everything but the tip of my cock. Pulling out at the last second, I come in jets onto her skirt.

I have to lick my lips and grip the edges of the counter, trying not to double over from the amount of oxygen I just lost. My gaze falls to the three melting containers of ice cream next to us.

We never did make it to that third flavor.

20

The football completely soared past my head, landing in a bush just feet away.

"Really, Bryan? Asshole." I shake my head, running to get it and whipping it back at him.

The ball hits him square in the chest, slipping through his fingers with a thud as the wind gets knocked out of him.

"Not cool, man. You could have bruised my lungs."

"Yeah, pretty sure that isn't a thing, and you're fine. Call someone else to kiss and make it better."

He wags his eyebrows. "Maybe I'll call Samantha. You know she likes me better dude."

Recently, my girlfriend had spent a rare night at my apartment, and Bryan had invited himself to be the third wheel no matter how many times I tried to signal that he was cock-blocking me. I finally had to tell him to get out or we were going to fuck right in front of him, and then he asked if I had popcorn. The bastard.

But I was glad that Samantha liked him, they had a similar humor and it was always nice when two of the most important people in your life got along.

"Keep dreaming, idiot."

My phone begins to ring, interrupting our immature measuring session.

"Hello?"

"Is this Jake Brady?"

The voice doesn't sound familiar. "Yes, it is, can I ask who's calling?"

"This is Melinda Harkness from the Foodie Conglomerate. I'm not sure if you've heard of us, but we saw your truck at the festival last month and were very impressed. After speaking with your marketing associate, we would like to pose to you the idea of opening up a retail storefront here in DC."

Ringing. In my ears. That must be it. Because she could not possibly have said what I thought she just said.

She can't have possibly just said what I think she said.

"I ... I know who you are. I'm sorry, I'm usually better at speaking on a professional level, or at all, but I'm a little in shock."

Great, I sound like some eight-year-old fan boy meeting Captain America. She's going to pull the deal from me.

Melinda laughs. "No worries at all, Jake, I understand what a big deal it is. Hey, I can say that because I own the company who gives culinary artists their dreams."

Did she just call me a culinary artist? I may spin around in a circle like a girl who was just asked to prom by her crush.

"Thank you for understanding." I clear my throat, trying to be a little more professional. "So how does this process work? What do you need from us? Where do we go from here?"

Melinda chuckles again. "Well, let's set up an intro meeting first, and we can answer all of those questions. I'll have the most important parts of our staff, designers and marketing and business planners, in on the meeting so that we can start discussing everything from paint colors to social media strategy. We are very interested in Cones & Corks ... and think it has a lot of potential."

My mind was like a speeding train, almost swerving off the tracks. There were so many thoughts, so many ideas that had been sitting dormant, and now I could finally dare to think about them.

"That sounds great. When works best for you?" I could barely think about the words I was forcing myself to speak.

Bryan was looking at me like I was standing in the middle of the park humping a monkey. My face probably looked insane, and I wouldn't be surprised if I was shaking like a leaf.

"I'll have my assistant email you to set something up. We're looking forward to this, Jake. Have a great weekend."

"You too, thank you." I can barely process anything, and have a hard time functioning to even hang up the phone.

I have to call Alice. I have to call Samantha. I have to slam a shot or fuck the shit out of my girlfriend. There is so much adrenaline pumping through my system right now that I don't know what to do.

"Dude, did you just win the lottery or something? Or did someone die? Shit ... that is insensitive of me. Fuck, uh ... are you okay?" Bryan won't stop rambling, as he tends to do, and a cackle starts in the back of my throat.

I start laughing like a lunatic, and I'm pretty sure people in the park are beginning to stare. Jamming my fingers to my phone, I quickly call the one person who will freak out as much as I am.

After three rings I get her voicemail. "This is Alice. If you're going to give me money, kindly leave a message. If you're just trying to be friendly, fuck off."

Jesus, good thing I made her get that second cell phone for business calls. Lord only knows how she would have screwed us out of a restaurant deal with a voicemail like that.

"Hey weirdo, call me back ASAP."

I hang up, needing to do a cartwheel or something to burst out the amount of energy coursing through my system.

"*Helloooo*?" Bryan snaps his fingers in front of my face.

"We are getting a storefront ..." I trail off, imagining the lines of people standing out front, waiting to try our latest creation.

"What?" While my friend is supportive, he knows absolutely nothing about the business.

"A group of restaurant investors wants to give Cones & Corks its own store ... we'd have our own location to serve customers from seven days a week instead of just the trucks."

I sit, suddenly feeling dizzy. I'm like a damsel in distress ... only everything is bright and shiny and I'm a hairy man.

"Seriously?! That's awesome. So when does it open?" He sits beside me, lounging so that his face is turned toward the sun.

I really want Alice to call me back so that we can start discussing, but part of me seizes up when Bryan asks that question. It's going to take a lot of time and hard work, decisions and compromises and working with construction crews.

There is even a chance it won't happen. I've talked to plenty of restaurant owners in this city who almost didn't even make it off the ground, and those who failed inside a year. Doubt begins to creep in, and now I kind of don't want to talk about ... don't want to jinx it.

"Well, we have to sit down and have a meeting first. Plenty of meetings actually ... I'm sure we'll meet with designers and marketing teams, not to mention the financial aspect of it. They may only give us a certain amount to play with. It's all kind of up in the air, and while it's good, there is a chance a store could never come to fruition."

I downplay my excitement, because my words are true. I have to be smart about this. If there is anything I've learned from being the black sheep of my family, it's that you never reveal your cards until all of the hands are dealt. So until I'm standing under the Cones & Corks sign outside of our store, I'm not going to get my hopes up.

"Still man, this shit is exciting. Hey, maybe I can finally work for you? Store Manager Bryan, that has a nice ring to it you gotta admit." He elbows me.

"Yeah, I think not. You can have one free cone a week ... that's it. I've got a business to run."

He pouts and starts to talk about loyalty, but I tune him out.

It feels like my life just turned a major corner, and I don't know if I'm going to walk away free floating, or smack into a closed door just on the other side.

"This is *not* on your road trip mix." I can't help but laugh as Jake notches the volume higher.

He gives me a quick glimpse before turning back to the highway and completely belting out a line of "Total Eclipse of the Heart."

"This is a classic, sing your heart out song ... and so yes, it is on the playlist. Don't judge me, you probably have Radio Disney or something in your CD player."

I sip some of my iced coffee and put it back in the cup holder. "Easy with the mommy jokes, stud. And for your information, when Lennon does get out of the car, I have Notorious B.I.G. on repeat."

"Of course you do." Jake rests his right hand on my thigh, his left arm commanding the wheel of his truck in a cocksure, sexy manner.

We pass a sign telling us we've just left Pennsylvania, and I'm into territory that I've never ventured to before. You would think that growing up on the East Coast, I would have visited the Big Apple, or somewhere close to it. But I've never been more north of Connecticut, and the only time I visited there, I was visiting

Mystic Pizza because mom was obsessed with the movie and dad wanted to give her the trip.

I placed my hand over his where it rested on my jeans, opening the window to breathe in a little of that northern air. It smelled more like fall up here, the last days of August passing through our fingers. Jake was taking me upstate, to his childhood home in Buffalo. I may have been through a lot of stuff in my life, but I was still as nervous as a sixteen-year-old high schooler going to her crush's house to meet his parents. His family was opening a new dealership and he was apparently expected to be there.

And while he hadn't explicitly said it, I could see the tension in the lines on his face. Could feel it in his body language. I was just hoping we could both escape unscathed and spend the rest of the weekend how we planned ... at a bed and breakfast on Seneca Lake, touring wineries. Nothing like drunk sex in the last days of summer alone with your boyfriend.

I laugh quietly, thinking about how lucky I am in this moment. I thought I'd had my great love, the one that I'd spent years on and came out with nothing. As a twenty-seven-year-old, I knew that was a depressing train of thought. But when you're a single mom, sometimes it feels like nothing in your life will ever be normal again. Like you won't get the traditional happily ever after because you've skipped a few steps and life doesn't like when you veer off course.

"Thanks for coming, babe. I'm just happy to get you all to myself."

I picked up the magazine I'd brought for reading ... some trashy tabloid that I couldn't get enough of. "I'm happy to have a little vacation, and I guess it's better that it's with you. Do you know that this is the first time I've taken a trip without Lennon?"

Jake changes lanes. "You're in dire need of it then, I'd say.

Maybe I'll even show you my childhood bedroom ... nothing like fucking on a squeaky twin bed."

His eyebrows go up and down suggestively, and I can't help but stare at him. Jesus, he's pretty. With that strong jaw, that dimple, the hair like a golden Adonis that is rumpled like I just held on tight. Like that night in the kitchen at his office.

I flush at the thought of the way we went at each other, groping and grinding like animals. Shit, it was so hot. Things in the sex department were the best I'd ever had, and when it came to the connection between our personalities, it was like I'd found a spark I'd been waiting a long time for. His relationship with Lennon had blossomed too, and she was getting more used to him being around the apartment. It had been a few months since we'd been seeing each other, and I felt like after this weekend, we were going to take another step. Going away together as a couple was a big deal ... add meeting someone's family in there, and it was huge.

"What is the weirdest thing you've ever done in a car?" I ask randomly, bored with already being in the car for two and a half hours.

"As in ... sex? I'm not sure how weird you can get in a car but—"

I put my hand over his mouth. "While I am kind of curious what the rest of that sentence might be, I don't need to hear about any sex besides the kind that happens between you and me. No, I mean, are you one of those people who clips their toenails while driving? Or something else odd or weird?"

Jake snorts, and tilts his head like he's thinking. "Yeah ... okay. This one time I was driving one of the trucks around the neighborhoods, early days of the business, and I got hungry. I typically won't eat the ice cream on a route, I feel like I'm losing myself money or something. So I saw that one of the guys had left some bread and peanut butter in the middle of the seats ... and while driving, I made myself a peanut butter sandwich."

"You couldn't have just pulled over?" I smile at his goofy expression.

"Time is money, baby. And I am a good multi-tasker, especially with my hands. I think you have seen that work in action."

"God, you're cheesy." I lean my seat back a little, impatient on long car rides.

"How about you? What's the craziest car ride story in your arsenal?"

I know exactly what the tale is, but blush before I go into it. "Okay, you should know that it was bumper to bumper traffic, and even though its unsafe, I was totally being as careful as I could."

"Why am I worried to hear this story now?" Those green eyes meet mine briefly.

I wave him off. "So this one day in Seattle, I got caught in the worst traffic. I'm talking not moving for *hours* at a time. And at first it was okay, because Lennon was asleep in the back peacefully. But then she woke up, and she started wailing. Crying bloody murder ... I thought she was going to shatter my eardrums. And I knew she was hungry so ... so I went back and unbuckled her and brought her up front. And I ... I started breastfeeding her. She quieted right down! That was all she wanted, and we still hadn't moved. But then I made eye contact with the guy in the car next to me, and I swear, he was staring so hard at my boobs that my nipples might as well have turned to him and waved hi."

Jake begins to laugh, the sound high and loud. "You really gave him a show? It was breast-to-breast traffic!"

I crack up too. "I swear, he was so interested in my breastfeeding that he almost hit the car in front of him."

"A tit and run!" Jake slaps the steering wheel, and we dissolve into a fit of laughter.

"So yeah, that's my weird car story. I totally topped yours, we need to have you do something strange on this road trip."

He adjusts his body in the seat. "I know one thing I haven't gotten while driving ..."

Glancing down, my eyes grow bigger when I see the tent he has going in his pants.

"If I put my mouth on that, it might be a moving violation."

We both laugh, the song changing on the radio to "Paradise by the Dashboard Light."

"You planned that, didn't you?" I take another sip of my coffee.

"If Meatloaf insists ..." He winks, taking an exit for another highway.

We fall into a contented silence, both of us singing a few words here and there. I read my magazine and text Mom for a while, her sending me half blurry pictures of Lennon running around.

"So tell me again about your family ... how many siblings do you have?"

Jake sighs, and I know I've broached a subject that he's been trying to avoid. "Three siblings, two brothers and a sister. I'm the youngest, so of course I was always the one who got picked on."

"And they all live in the same town? I've always wondered what that would be like, to live one place your whole life, surrounded by family." At times, I thought it actually sounded pretty nice. Everything was familiar, people knew your family and your name.

"It's boring and settled, trust me. Sure, I guess it could be comforting in some sense, but none of my brothers or sister have ever worked for anything. They graduated, were paid for to go to college, and then handed a position in the family business. When it came my turn, I just ... I couldn't do it."

I'm not sure what to say, because clearly this is a sticking point with him. I want to be supportive, but I also want to give his family a chance.

Jake clears his throat, apparently done with talking about the family we are driving almost seven hours to go see.

"How about you, are you an only child? I've never seen anyone else at Molly's house for the couple of years I've been driving around her neighborhood."

That makes me sad ... and a little guilty that I was away on the other side of the country for so many years. I took her for granted sometimes, but Mom was probably thrilled that we were living back in the DC metro area.

"My brother, Charlie, is actually in Africa, saving lives. Little bro always did have to outshine me ... just kidding, I love him, but we haven't seen each other much in the last couple of years. And then my dad ... he died when I was a teenager. I don't think Mom has really ever been able to completely move on from it, although I would absolutely be supportive of her finding someone to make her happy."

"Oh shit, Samantha, I'm ... I didn't know. I'm sorry."

"You don't have to be, he was an amazing dad. I was lucky to have the time I did with him."

Jake clears his throat, his hand finding mine where it rests on the other side of the car. "If it makes you feel better, I can commiserate. I lost my mom when I was ten."

Tears fill my eyes, and I blink them away. All this time we'd been seeing each other, and neither of us knew that we had way more in common than we'd imagined.

"I guess that just makes us two members of the same club no one wants to be in, huh?"

He nods, and I can't help but lean over and kiss his cheek,

my lips lingering there, my nose soaking in his clean, minty scent.

"It's weird, but ever since we met ... well, *again*, I've felt a deeper connection with you than almost anyone I've come across in my life. Maybe there is a truth to saying that souls seek out other souls they find similar."

Now emotion clogs my throat. "That is beautiful. And I think you're right."

I kept his fingers laced in mine but sat back in the passenger seat, content to know that I was with someone who, even before I knew him, already shared so many of the same life experiences.

And now I was thinking that maybe it wasn't just happenstance after all that led me to moving back home.

One of the things I actually appreciate about home is being surrounded by a ton of voices; the chaos and familiarity still make me feel some sense of belonging.

Kids run around the front yard of the big McMansion my father bought about ten years ago at the insistence of my stepmother, Shelly. They throw balls, ride around on motorized toys, all while their two golden retrievers chase them. My sister, Kelly, pushes a stroller around the driveway, watching the two toddlers who play around with chalk on the blacktop.

My brothers shoot the shit on the porch, sipping beers while my dad stands on the front steps, looking over his empire. There may be some tension, but I always enjoy coming home. At least for a few hours, before everyone starts in on each other and we all get sick as shit of one another.

"Samantha, what is it that you do again?" Ian, my middle brother, asks.

"I work for the National Parks Service. I started there in Seattle, and just recently moved back to DC."

"West Coast, huh? Nothing like the best coast. We took a trip out there to wine country last year for our anniversary, it was awesome. Jake, you have no idea what good wine is until you've been out there." Michael plants a smug smile on his face.

I want to point out that Napa Valley is nowhere close to Seattle, and that my brother has no idea what the West Coast is like as he has barely left Buffalo, but I keep my trap shut. With each word my brothers speak, I feel it grate on my nerves. I just needed to get through the next day and a half, and then it was smooth sailing up to the wineries and lakes with the gracious woman holding my hand.

"And Samantha has a daughter, Lennon." I pull out a phone and show them a selfie of Lennon and I with a Snapchat filter that makes us look like we have tomatoes on our head.

Ian raises his eyebrows. "Oh, I didn't realize that. How old is she?"

Michael's wife, Denise, walks up to our group and begins to listen. "She's three, going on thirty. It really is true when they say that little girls are like teenagers."

"Oh, you're a mother? I hadn't realized. Is your daughter in school, do you practice organic? Are you into any of those anti-vaccination things?"

The questions were strange and Samantha laughed a little, a nervous tone coming out of her mouth. I laced my fingers through hers to let her know I was there, but this was just plain weird. Why was it that women were constantly trying to compete with each other?

Hell, I could answer that ... seeing as my brothers and I were constantly competing for everything from Dad's love to who had the nicer car.

"Just a regular old mom. Not one of those fancy ones who seems to have time to pose in priceless outfits for professional photos that she posts on Instagram. I never can quite grasp how they do it, I can barely vacuum my area rug and I live in a thousand square foot apartment. Meanwhile these ladies have immaculate white kitchens and fire pits with marble stools."

Michael and Ian look at each other, then look at Michael's wife. The expression on her face is a sour one, and I swallow the laugh that is about to come out of my throat, causing me to make some kind of choking bird noise.

I should have remembered that Denise was one of those Instagram famous mommies.

"Some of us believe that raising your children in a healthy, beautiful, cultured environment influences them to grow up to be stronger, more worldly people." Denise sniffs in Samantha's direction, as if a cockroach might crawl out from under her hair.

"Oh, I'm sorry ... I didn't mean—" Samantha sputters, and I am about to jump in until someone farther down the porch shouts.

"Dinner! Come in and wash your hands, children, and sit in your assigned seats." Shelly came out, her diamond studs flashing in the setting sun.

We are literally saved by the dinner bell.

Forks scrape, mouths chew, bowls are passed and chatter runs on endlessly from the thirty person dinner table in the immaculate dining room Shelly and my father have created.

I'm not sure why I was put to the right of my father, but my brothers were looking at me like I'd pissed in their Cheerios. Looking at the old man, I realize he did look older than the last time I'd seen him about eight months ago. His hair, once the same golden brown as mine, was mostly gray at this point. His face, while still what most would consider handsome, is lined with wrinkles and a constant stern expression. My father has never been a particularly warm man, and his harsh business persona often carried over into his personal life.

"I'm glad you wised up and decided to come home for the new dealership opening. Having the whole family intact for this was one of my dreams ... not to mention your mothers."

Ah, so we were using the dead mom card tonight to guilt, good to know.

"Glad to do it, it's been a while. Not that I know my Ford from my Hyundai." I shrug, throwing the little jab in there just because I can.

Samantha stops chewing next to me, and I know she can hear the tension in my voice. It's funny how well she knows me after just a few months, when my entire life, it's like I've never quite fit into the puzzle that is the Brady family. If I had to come here, had to put myself through this, I'm glad she's here with me. Part of me hopes I'm showing her the vulnerable part of myself, just like she's allowed me to become a part of Lennon's life.

"Maybe you guys can come down for the food truck festival next year ... you know you still haven't seen my trucks." I cut into my piece of steak, and fork a cube of meat. I need to change the subject, and maybe if I do this for them, they'll finally come and see my business.

In the years since I'd opened Cones & Corks, none of my family members have come to visit and see how well I was doing. In fact, they barely contacted me down south, a fact that still ate at me.

"Because we have a real business to run up here, son. We don't have time for vacations or ice cream." Dad ribs Michael, who then laughs and makes a face at Ian.

"Actually, Dad, I've had my own successful business for three years, and we just got picked up to open a retail space." I could feel my blood pressure rising.

"You did, eh? Well, send us an invite to the opening, we'll see if it comes to fruition." He didn't even look up, just kept chewing his dinner. "So, Kelly, how are the salesmen at the Waterloo dealership doing?"

And that was it. Just like that he fucking dismissed me, choosing to talk about some bumfuck branch of his business.

Samantha leans to me, her hand on my leg taking me down a notch. "Do you want to get some air?"

The conversation continues on around us, and I nod, not able to stomach this charade any longer. I get up, the table looking at me, and simply walk out. They didn't give a shit about what I had to say just seconds ago, so what was the point of explaining myself now?

Once outside on the porch, I blew out a breath and slammed my fist into the railing a couple of times. My blood still curdled in my ears, all of the things I'd like to say on the tip of my tongue.

"Would it have been better if I blew up at them?" I hear her come out behind me, her toned arms wrapping around my waist as she presses herself against my back.

"We could go back in there, I could get in a mommy fight with Denise and you could battle your father?"

I chuckled under my breath, bitterness tangy on my tongue.

Samantha kissed my back. "But no, I don't think it would do any good. Sometimes we just have to swallow the bitter pill and know that we are in the right ... even when you want to claw someone's eyes out. Fuck them, you know?"

Hearing the curse word come out of her mouth makes me finally turn, staring down at her and taking her face in my hands. Just feeling her skin was like a balm to my salted wounds, and I could feel my heart opening in a way it never had before. Sure, it sounded so unmanly, but I was falling for this incredible woman and I didn't care to hide it.

"How come you didn't tell me about the retail store?" The moonlight streams through her dark hair.

I shrug, suddenly feeling shy. "I'm not sure ... I wanted to feel like it was, real or something, first. I didn't want to jinx anything, and it still could fall through. Was it too much to ask to bring you in when everything was done and knock you on your ass?"

We both smile at my attempt at a joke, and she snuggles into my chest so that we don't have to make eye contact in this moment. I think she senses that it's getting too heavy.

"I'd love to hear more about it when you're ready ... and I'll even help pick paint colors. I'm good at that."

Everything in me wants to stay out here, alone with her. My body recoils at going back inside, at staying until tomorrow to stand up on the podium at the dealership like some good politician's son.

"You know what? Let's get out of here." Saying the decision out loud only confirmed it in my head as the right thing to do.

Samantha pulled back, her expression not negative but curious. "But what about tomorrow? And your family?"

I shook my head, trying to flesh out my thoughts. "They'll always be my family, but sometimes family is wrong. If they can't support me, why should I stick around to do so for them? I don't need that kind of negativity in my life. And we can take one more day to escape reality, go to the bed and breakfast early. If we leave now, we can get there before closing."

She titled her head, her tongue darting out to wet her lips. "Well then, what are we waiting for?"

Move of a hip.
SQUEAK.
Thrust of a thigh.
SQUEAK.

"I can't concentrate like this." I collapse onto Jake's chest, a fit of giggles and moans mixing together in my delirious state.

"I can get you to concentrate ..." Jake inches his hips up, his cock hitting the exact spot inside of me that makes stars appear in front of my retinas.

"Everyone in this hallway can hear us!" I whisper shout, giggling again but my orgasm is so close to the brink that I feel like I'm going insane.

We've been making love on and off throughout the night, the first time being as soon as we stepped inside this room at the bed and breakfast so that Jake could work off the steam he collected in his ears at his father's house. From there we would wake up every two to three hours, unable to stop our fingers from trailing over each other's skin.

And now the sun was coming through the curtains, and we

could hear the rustle of people as they awoke inside the Victorian house. The king bed in our room may as well have been made from rusty brake pads it was so noisy, and the closer we got to coming, the worse the sounds got. I think everyone in this hotel knew what position—girl on top—we were in and how deep Jake was inside of me.

"So let them, nosy fuckers." Jake moves, one hand clasped on the back of my neck so that he can raise my head up to meet his blazing green eyes.

Oh, good God. I can't possibly worry about anything else but the orgasm wracking my system when he looks like that.

We come in a flurry of shouts, squeaks and the headboard hitting the wall.

"I think we might have broken the bed." He chuckles, his hands smoothing over every inch of my skin as if he's trying to catalogue it.

"Hey, we had to make use of it if we were paying for an extra night, I think we really got our money's worth." I blew a few stray strands of hair out of my face and propped my chin on his chest.

"Do you think it's time for this world class brunch I've been reading about?"

Jake had picked this resort for its close proximity to a few Seneca Lake wineries he wanted to check out for distribution deals, and because the breakfast was raved about on TripAdvisor. I guess it really was true that the way to a man's heart was through his stomach. It sat on an estate that was only visible once you crested the long winding road up. An old Victorian house with charm and modern fixtures, the whole resort sat on these beautiful gardens that looked straight out of an English palace, backing right up to the edge of Seneca Lake. It was completely romantic and rustic ... and I think we were both beginning to fall under its spell.

"Can we even show our faces at brunch?" A blush spreads over my cheeks.

"Get up. I'm taking you for some eggs Benedict, baby." He slaps my butt, the sound probably resonating in the hall through these paper thin walls.

Thirty minutes later and we're showered, in our winery best, scarfing down the most delicious spread of eggs, waffles, muffins and sizzling bacon I've ever laid eyes on.

Sure, there are some weird looks thrown our way from other guests, but Jake flashes them that dimple and waves, and I'm in a fit of giggles again.

After we finish, our stomachs full, it's time to get drunk. Well ... at least for me it is. Jake keeps calling this a business trip, but I'm just here to taste a lot of wine while I have a hall pass from being a parent. With an expert sommelier, who also happened to be very sexy and nice to look at, this was the ultimate pleasure trip.

A shuttle from the B&B took us to our first winery, a small family owned place that was shaped like a barn and had a black Labrador laying on the front steps. Jake spent most of this visit speaking with the owner, trading business tips and then we sampled a couple of their wines. They had a strawberry-based wine that was to die for, and I raved about it until Jake promised he'd make a strawberry flavored ice cream.

A little tipsy, and pulling up to our next stop on the tour, I rest my head on Jake's shoulder. My nose is tingling, which is how I know I'm on my way to drinking too much. But the sun is out, we're "working" for his business, and I'm happier than I've been in years.

Walking up to one of the counters in the next winery, a big operation type of place with beautiful rooms and windows for walls that show visitors the entire property, Jake chats with the employee, who sets two glasses on the counter.

"Okay, let's challenge your palette a little." The employee, a larger, Hispanic looking guy, smirks at Jake.

He clearly wants to stump him. He pours us each three glasses of white and three glasses of red ... of which I get started on immediately. I have no manners or etiquette when it comes to all the swishing, sniffing and spitting. I gulp 'em down, loving every delicious taste.

Jake takes about twenty minutes to get through all of his glasses, and then looks up at the guy. He may not be smiling, but I know that cocky gleam in his eye.

"From left to right ... merlot, dry cabernet, and you tried to trick me with this one, but the last red is a shiraz. As far as the whites, you should have tried harder ... chardonnay blend, dry Riesling, and a Gewürztraminer."

The employee tips a fake hat in Jake's direction and I look up at him dreamily, the wine infusing my blood.

"Let's take a walk, Tipsy." Jake's big hand settles on the curve of my back and he walks me to the entrance.

We find our way to the vineyard, walking among the tall leaves curving up towards the sky. My hand rests in his, the peace of this afternoon mixing with the wine running through my veins.

"Do you regret leaving last night?" I ask because I do feel kind of bad that we left his family sitting at the dinner table.

I can just imagine Denise's face ... I would pay money to see that.

"Honestly? No. Is it bad to say that I haven't even thought of it until now? I'm not even sure why I agreed to go to the opening in the first place. Some disingenuous, delusional sense of loyalty I guess."

I nodded, seeing his point. "I've always dreamed of having a big family, but ... and I don't mean this in a malicious way, last night kind of sucked. For people who have so much, the atmosphere in the room portrayed anything but."

Jake takes my hand and walks me through the rows, picking up a grape leaf here or there and examining it. "I don't take offense, the way my family behaves ninety percent of the time is atrocious."

We're silent for a minute, walking along the rows, tall stalks of wine grapes hiding us. The sunlight streams through every so often, but out here, it could be just us two and the world melts away.

"Sometimes you just have to settle with the fact that not everyone is going to want the best for you, even if that is your family. It's been a long time coming, but I think something clicked last night. How am I supposed to believe in myself, in my choices in life, if I'm always looking backward for approval? I don't need it, and I think that piece of the puzzle revealed itself to me at that dinner table. We choose who we let in, and how they affect us."

His words were off the cuff, but so wise. I'd thought for so long that I needed to make things work with Derek because that was what society or fate or whatever had taught me ... when really, my daughter and I were in a much healthier place without him.

"I love you."

The words come out of my mouth before I mean for them to, but once they're out there, I don't feel any of that rush to take them back. No embarrassment of saying them to a man first, or panic because I didn't really mean them.

It had taken me years before to get comfortable with saying those three little words. But as I'd said from the first time I was reintroduced to Jake ... there was something between us. Something that wasn't complicated or hard-to-get, and from there we'd just progressed. I never had to guess what he was thinking, or second guess myself to wonder if we were on the same page. There was honesty and maturity here, and out of that, I'd grown to love him quickly. Watching him with my daughter, how he treated my own feelings with such care ... it was no wonder I'd fallen head over heels in just a short amount of time.

Jake has stopped walking, and just stares at me, a little smirk on his face that makes that dimple pop.

"How smart am I that I got the girl I crushed on hard in college to fall in love with me?" His hands move to my hips, the heat of them shooting straight through my thin cotton sundress and sending goose bumps over my skin.

"How do you know I'm not just drunk?" I make a study out of his green eyes.

"Because I know you. And I love you, too."

The shock I expected to come from saying the words myself, comes when Jake says them. He utters them so matter-of-factly, as if they've been between us forever. The expression on his face is warm, his cheeks relaxed into a smile, his eyes adoringly capturing me.

"You do?" While my mind is clear, my tongue is tipsy with wine.

He nods. "You should know I've never said those words to anyone else. Which I guess makes me a virgin. But in any case, I do love you. And I love Lennon. I know it hasn't been that long, but there is that corny saying about knowing when you know. And I just know."

It was simple and uncomplicated ... a refreshing change from the past. While there were still kinks to work out, hell life always had kinks, my heart dared to soar.

"Well now that we got *that* out of the way," I winked at him, "let's go have some real fun. More wine!"

"Don't I get a kiss? Or maybe I can cop a feel? I've always had this fantasy about being alone in a vineyard ..."

Jake's hand trailed down to cup my ass, and I squealed, but the noise was swallowed by expert lips capturing my own. Now *this* was the fun part I was talking about.

24

SAMANTHA

Hundreds of people flooded the lawn, blankets spread and chairs propped, snacks waiting to be demolished. Kids ran screaming, playing with new friends they'd just met or skipping as their parents took photos.

And for once, I was a part of one of these couples. I had someone on my blanket to laugh at Lennon with, who took pictures and texted them to me so I could post them on Facebook. Who wrapped his arms around me when the breeze came in, as they rolled the projector screen down and everyone clapped for the impending start of the movie.

"This was a great idea, babe." I turned my head back, tilting to see him as we sat, my back to his chest.

"What can I say? I'm a regular at this ole date planning thing." He shrugs, looking like the picture of innocence.

"Except for that first time, huh?"

"Never going to let me live that one down, are you?"

"Never." I nuzzle into him, waiting for the kiss that gets planted on my cheek.

"I love you, babe," Jake whispers in my ear, his voice tickling my skin.

Ever since our trip to New York, and our confessions among the vines, he's been saying it more and more. The first time he did, he reminded me that he wanted to say it while I wasn't laced with drink, and then called me a booze hound. I'd never heard anything so romantic.

"Me cuddle too!" Lennon jumps on us, her foot digging into my ribs as she climbs my body to get to Jake.

"Who let the gorilla into the movies?" Jake lifts her off me, moving us out of our snuggling position, and cradles her. "Oo, oo, ah, ah, ah!"

Lennon pretends to speak in a monkey language back to him as he tickles her.

"Mommy, I hope we watching *Cinderella*." Her dark curls are everywhere as she looks at me upside down from her place in Jake's arms.

"Oh, sweet pea, it's actually called *Inside Out* ... but don't worry, I think you'll like it."

"*Inside Out! Inside Out!*" She claps her hands, chanting for the movie to start.

Luckily, we're outside and every other person around us has screaming toddlers too, or I'd be embarrassed. Except for this younger group of kids ... well teenagers I should say, that are seated a little behind us. They're all acting way too cool to be here, yet it's probably the only safe place for freedom without parents that their mothers and fathers would allow them to go on a Saturday night.

"Remember when you were that cool?" I jerk my thumb to their group.

Jake settles Lennon in his lap, and she happily rests against him. I think my heart literally turns to mush in that moment.

"Oh, hell yeah, I was the leader of the pack at that age. Wore the backwards hat, flirted with the girls after the bell rang, fist bumped all my dudes when we snuck a six-pack of Bud Heavy below the bleachers."

"And so humble too, I bet that's why they all liked you." I rolled my eyes at him.

"Come on, you would have had *such* a crush on me in high school." He leaned over, his dimple seducing me, as he lightly kissed me.

"Yuck!" Lennon broke us up by shoving her hands in my mouth.

Pretending to eat them, I gobbled at her fingers until she laughed.

The screen lit up, and a little cartoon about the concession stand began to play. And then Joy, or my girl Amy Poehler, came onto the screen, introducing the emotions to the park full of silent movie goers, the summer darkness swallowing us.

"She's falling asleep already." Jake held my hand while Lennon grabbed onto his other fingers.

I chewed on a Twizzler and looked over, my ovaries practically batting their eyelashes as my daughter turned my boyfriend into a big teddy bear.

A really freaking handsome, stud of a teddy bear. The nineteen forties movie star good looks, the swooping golden brown hair, the arms that I wanted to grope every time I saw them. Those green eyes that always held a hint of mischief, not to mention what lay underneath the powder blue T-shirt and jeans he had on tonight. Damn ... I could stare at Jake all day.

"Good, maybe we'll get an entire movie to ourselves ... albeit a kid's one," I whisper back, leaning my head on his shoulder.

Half of the movie goes by, some groups getting up to leave with cranky children or just because the temperature was dropping. We stayed, enjoying the peace and quiet as Lennon slept softly in Jake's lap.

"Mmmmm ..." A sound comes from behind us, a moan.

I ignore it, choosing to focus on the hot headed emotion in the movie. I related to him at times, wanting to curse people out and being silenced by another emotion that was too powerful and telling anger to be quiet.

"Oh my God ..." Another sound, and I'm turning my head.

And I have to stifle a surprised gasp when I look over. The group of teens is paired off, about four couples in all, each snuggling under a blanket.

Except ... they're not watching the movie *at all*.

"Babe ..." I hiss at Jake, pointing back so he looks subtly behind us.

He can't stop the howl of laughter, and someone around us shushes him. "Well, at least someone is getting their rocks off at this movie."

The blankets are moving, most of the kids making out while things are going on, down there.

"Should we stop them? They're just doing this completely out in public. There are kids here!" I'm half-appalled, half-impressed. They have some balls, pun intended, to slide into third base right here in the middle of this family friendly movie night.

"Honey, let them be kids. Honestly, it's probably not even that good. They're getting below average hand jobs ... let them live their glory days. Our girl is asleep, and we are having an uninterrupted date night. Pick your battles."

He was kind of right, and the fact that he'd just called Lennon "our girl" was distracting me from the amateur sexual acts going on behind us.

"Do you think they even know where a clit is?" I giggle, settling back into him.

"Couldn't find it with a road map and a compass ... not that they'd know how to use those either. They'd need Google Maps for the genitally challenged."

I burst out a laugh and someone shushes us again. "Why don't you let me give you a below average hand job when we get home?"

"Baby, I'll let you pop my cherry any night of the week."

25

"Okay, we have popcorn, ice cream, cotton candy and Cracker Jacks. If there is anything else you can possibly fit in that stomach of yours, then I don't know what we'll feed you because I think you ate this stadium out of concessions."

I give Lennon a funny look as I hold all of the treats in my arms, settling back into the seats reserved for us.

"She's got Natitude!" Bryan sticks his tongue out and tickles Lennon, and her curls shake as she laughs.

"Ice cream please!" Her little smile could convince me of anything.

I thought taking this little girl for the day would give Samantha a nice break. My girlfriend rarely got time to herself, and with me now in the picture, that was even less. She deserved a day off to get her nails done or her hair lightened, or whatever it was that women did when they were single for a day.

But I never realized just how much I'd worry. I'd made Lennon hold my hand from the minute we left the car in the parking garage, not to mention how I drove here with the speed of a grandpa since she was sitting in the backseat of the car.

When she'd wanted to wander to see the mascot outside the Nationals ball park, I'd gripped tight and picked her up, making sure she couldn't wiggle out of my arms. Once inside, I understood why some parents used those leashes. She was so tiny among the sea of legs around her, and I couldn't imagine the ways I'd lose my mind if she got lost. I'd brought Bryan with me because we loved baseball, and the Nationals ... and I needed moral support. If I wasn't able to watch her, to say, go get all of the concessions she wanted, he could keep an eye on her. Not that I trusted Bryan much more than the three-year-old he was tasked with watching ... they pretty much had the same emotional maturity.

Handing her the ice cream in a mini-baseball cap, I steal a spoonful. "Let me just test it first. Mmm, that's good."

"Mine, Jake!" She takes it from me and sets it on her lap, and I just know she's going to drop something down the little team shirt I'd gifted her just days before.

"Say thank you." I gave her a stern look, trying to channel Samantha. She made being a parent look easy ... when in reality, today I was probably undoing all the good she'd done thus far.

"Thank you!" Her cute little voice and smile melt me as she blinks up, chocolate ice cream smeared across her mouth.

"I think that kid is even more charming than you." Bryan leans over her, Lennon sitting between us, her little legs dangling off the seat.

"Oh I know she is." I tune into the game, already in the second inning.

No one tells you that kids also become the first priority. I'd come thinking we'd catch the entire game, and I'd be able to see the boys deliver a bruising to the Orioles. Instead, it had taken us double the time to make it into the stadium, because Lennon wanted to take pictures with the mascot and look at all of the kid's attractions that the park had set up for game day. Then she'd had to go to the bathroom, so instead of just unzipping and pissing in the urinal like I would normally, I had to take her into a stall with me and help her go. By the time we'd made it to our section, she wanted a snack. And pushover me, I gave in when she asked for all of them.

She was just too cute ... like bachelor kryptonite. I couldn't say no, honestly, I had no idea how the beautiful woman I was dating ever said no to her daughter.

A Nationals player steps up to the plate, getting into his batting stance and eyeing down the pitcher. The sun shines down on the field, the air warm but with a hint of that coolness of a changing season. There was something more magical about baseball in September, more on the line. The pitcher shakes off the catcher, deciding on the second call his partner makes, and straightens before he lets the ball loose. In a split-second, it's over the plate, and the crack reverberates around the stadium as our batter swings hard and connects.

"YEAH!" Bryan stands, watching the ball soar over the field.

"Go, go, go!" I stand too, my body in a weird crouching position to make sure Lennon doesn't need anything.

The entire stadium is biting their nails, except for the couple of Orioles fans sitting a couple rows back. The ball keeps going, our batter rounding the bases as he watches from the corner of his eye, making sure it goes over the wall. When it finally does, people erupt into clapping and shouting.

"Hell yeah! I mean ... heck yeah!" Bryan covers his mouth, glancing quickly at Lennon.

I high five my best friend and then shake my little girl's shoulders. "Home run, sweet pea!"

The Orioles fans behind us boo, and it must sound nice to Lennon, who has powered through the ice cream, because she imitates them. "*BOOO!*"

I sit down, laughing a little at her innocence. Her mother is so lucky I'm in her life now, to teach her the right sports teams to root for. How misguided they both have been.

"No, love ... we want to cheer for that. That's our team, and they scored a point! So say yay!" I raise my arms up in celebration.

She looks at me, curling her legs up into the seat and rocking so that the retractable chair almost swings up and swallows her. "Booo!"

"I guess we need to work on that." I roll my eyes, facing back to the field below and hooking my arm around her seat.

"Your daughter is adorable." An older couple in front of us turns back to smile at her.

I'm about to say she isn't mine, but something in their voices makes me soften too. I've spent a few months with this little human, and she's really grown on me. What I used to think would be impossible to handle, a situation way too big for my single ways, has become nothing but a fleeting thought. I never thought in the near future that I would be responsible for someone else's life, or the caring of another person. But Lennon, and Samantha, have changed my entire view. I care so much about her that I understood what it meant now to want to take a bullet for another person ... or wipe their butt after they pooped.

"Thanks!" Lennon leaned into my arm and smiled at them, her devilish little smile making me laugh.

"Thank you." I smooth a hand over her hair.

Bryan looked at me, his expression a mix of a question and one that said, "I'm impressed."

"Proud of you, buddy. Never thought I'd see the day."

I hand Lennon her cotton candy. "Says the eternal bachelor with the emotional capacity of a carrot."

"Well, we knew that about me. I just knew that you had more in you, if you opened up to it. They're good for you, you know."

"I know how lucky I am, trust me." I looked down at the little girl, a lion-like fierceness grabbing my heart.

I didn't just love her mom, I loved her too. It felt like a bottle being smashed on my heart, warm gooey liquid gushing out of the cracked center. For a long time, I'd been me, myself and I. And I'd always been fine with it. But now I wanted to make it official, I'd found people who I wanted in my life forever ... and it felt cheap to only be a side character. An idea began brewing in my head.

"YAY!" Lennon cheers when the crowd does, and I watch as one of our batters gets a double and sprints to second base.

"Hey, you're getting the hang of it." I reach down for a high five.

Now we were getting somewhere.

"W hen I grow up, I want to be a unicorn." Lennon chirps happily in Jake's arms, her chubby little hand touching his cheek.

It makes my heart squeeze, and then take off in double time. In just a matter of months, the two of them have bonded so spectacularly. And while I knew that we were taking things slow, and I didn't want to have the "where are we going with this" discussion, Jake was insane if he thought he didn't know how to handle kids.

"Well, you'll need to work on growing your horn a little, but I think it's a great dream." He taps her forehead and she giggles.

Case in point, he was a natural.

"What if mommy wants you to be a doctor, or a lawyer? We got bills to pay here, squirt." I ruffled her hair and moved over into Jake's side.

His warmth as he wrapped his free arm around my shoulder was addicting. Looking up, I caught one beautiful green eye, and he winked.

The elevator does slid open, and we walked out into the lobby of my building as a unit.

"That's boring, mommy! Maybe I be a farmer! I'll have chickens, cows, pumpkins, peacocks ..." My daughter trailed off, looking faraway and I knew she was imagining her future farm.

Jake leaned over to me. "I don't know what kind of farm has peacocks, but I'm not going to dash the kid's dreams."

We both quietly laughed. We were halfway across the lobby when a scruffy voice caught my ear.

"Surprise!"

I turn, not expecting to see Derek, all six-foot-two tattooed feet of him, leaning against the check in desk.

It had been months since I'd seen him, months since he'd seen his daughter, who was now resting comfortably in another man's arms.

I guess I was surprised when Lennon squirmed from Jake's arms and ran across the tile screaming "Daddy!"

He scooped her up, giving her kisses all over her cheeks. Derek had never been cold with our daughter, but he was more fun uncle than father figure.

I saw his eyes meet Jake over the top of Lennon's head, his lips turning down in ... what? Disapproval? Annoyance? Jealousy?

"Hey, Sammy. Good to see you." He walked over, our daughter still in his hands.

Inside, I'm weirdly relieved that I feel ... nothing towards him. Part of me felt like putting an entire country between us would help lessen the feelings I thought I still had for him. But with Jake standing next to me, I realized that the love I'd felt for Derek had been different. It was first time kind of love; special in it's own way, but after it burned out, I didn't feel any of the embers still sparking.

And it made all of the emotions that had been up in the air about Jake, firmly plant in my chest. Suddenly, I was sure that I was in love with him, in the mature, adult kind of way that didn't need to involve flowers, hearts and candy, but was just a fact.

"Hi, Derek ... I didn't realize you were coming into town. Jake, this is Lennon's father, Derek. Derek, this is Jake, my boyfriend." I didn't hesitate to say it, and didn't flinch when Derek's nostrils flared.

I tried to keep my composure, to not burst out right there in a fit of tiger mommy and scorned ex. He was the one who hadn't wanted us, who hadn't bothered to fight for neither me nor his daughter. And now he showed up here, months later after he'd cancelled every single visit he was supposed to have with Lennon, and put on this facade of a loving father and jealous former flame? Bitch, I didn't think so, hold my earrings.

My inner-badass was really raring for a fight, apparently.

Jake stuck out his hand. "Hey, man, nice to meet you. I've heard some great things from this one about her dad."

Lennon smiled and stuck her fingers in Derek's ear. "Daddy, take me to the park!"

Her innocence had me smiling, because thank God she wasn't traumatized from his absence.

"What do you say, Sammy, can I take her for the day? Or better yet, want to join us?" Something suspicious marked his tone.

I looked at Jake, silently trying to convey my apology for our day being ruined. Pumpkins and hayrides would have to wait. "Do you mind? We can all go along to the park?"

Jake kept his arm around me, his easy, comforting nature not being thrown off by this surprise arrival. "Not at all, Lennon has been wanting to feed the ducks anyway. She's only been talking about it all week."

He winked at Lennon, who giggled and screamed, "Ducks!"

"Then off we go, I guess. One big happy family." Derek's tone did not match his smirk, and in the pit of my stomach, a nauseous foreboding sense took flight.

Dark curl streamed through the crisp autumn air as my little girl shrieked and ran, throwing bread crumbs behind her to the ducks that now followed her path.

"I missed her a lot." Derek doesn't take his dark blue eyes off of her, his hand fisted in his beard.

He looks leaner than he did when I last saw him the night before we left Seattle, and there is something more grounded about him. It both scares me and makes me proud, because I had only spent a good decade of my life trying to get him to see his worth and potential. I guess that had been my downfall though, trying to change the man. Every story of dating gone wrong, movies, books or even TV shows, had taught women that you couldn't change a man who didn't want to change himself. So I guess I had made the right move in leaving, since clearly it wasn't me he had wanted to be different for.

"She misses you too ... but, Derek, what are you doing here?" I tried to make my tone as non-aggressive as possible.

His scowl tells me I don't quite pull it off. "Am I not allowed to see my daughter, Sammy?"

I hated that nickname now. "Of course you are, but ... we had so many trips planned for you to see her and you called them all off. I guess ... I just don't know why now, unplanned. I don't ... you know I never have a problem with you seeing her, I want you to be in her life. I just feel like this is out of left field."

"Why, because you're hiding your boyfriend on the other side of the country, playing house with him and our daughter?" His words are acid.

I face him, try to find anything familiar in his face from the man I know. "Come on, Derek, you know it's not like that. You were completely fine with me moving her here, we broke up and there were no hard feelings. I don't have to tell you who I'm dating, and you don't have to do me that courtesy either. Not that I'm hiding it, I'll answer any questions you have about Jake."

Jake runs to Lennon, scooping her up and flying her around like an airplane. I watch Derek watch them, his eyes becoming more fiery by the second. I'd forgotten that about him, his short temper. It wasn't often that I saw it, but when I did, I knew to steer clear.

"You don't have to do me the courtesy? Actually, since he seems to be spending nights at your place with our daughter in the next bedroom, I believe you do owe me that. Or at least, we could see what the court says about it."

The malice in his tone makes my heart drop, and even though we're sitting in a calm, serene park, I know Derek has the match to make my world go up in flames.

"We agreed that we wouldn't take this to court ..." I try not to let me voice crack.

We hadn't been married, weren't even engaged at any point. We were just two people who had a child together, and we'd agreed when I moved back to the East Coast that we would work any custody arrangements out between us. The word court struck fear in my body, made me want to go grab my daughter and run as far away as possible.

"Maybe we need to revisit that agreement then." His hands were fisted, the tattoos on them staring angrily at me.

My mouth goes dry as sweat simultaneously coats my back. Even in the cool fall air, I feel like I'm going to combust. Every-thing I've built here, all the time I've spent getting Lennon to re-adjust, the time I spent healing my own heart.

"Don't do this, Derek. Don't do this to her." My tone is pleading.

He stands and walks to where she's playing, not giving me a backward glance. Desperation and survival course through my veins as I watch the man of my past, and the one in my future, play with my daughter.

I try to breathe, and keep the tears inside as she runs to me, bringing me one of the last summer flowers she could find in the grass.

27

"You're pretty quiet, everything okay?"

I try to ease into the conversation, resting my hand on Samantha's leg across the console. Maneuvering my truck with one hand, I steer us towards my apartment, a rare night spent at my place while Lennon has a sleepover with Derek at his hotel.

She doesn't look at me, my gaze seeing nothing but long brown hair as my girl looks out the window of the truck at the dark night sky.

"Babe?" I shake her leg a little, needing for her to talk to me.

Her ex-boyfriend showing up today was a surprise, one that tilted our perfect little world off-kilter, leaving the status of what we were and who I was to Lennon up in the air.

"Sorry, I'm just ... digesting." Her smile doesn't reach her eyes when she looks over at me in the dim light of the car.

The day had a tenseness about it, an undertone that I couldn't joke away. Normally, I'd have laughed it off or played some goofy prank, anything to keep from getting too serious about everything. But with Derek dropping in, I knew this was serious. And I seriously didn't like that guy. What kind of father didn't see his child for close to six months, and then just waltzes in unexpectedly to claim glory and her love. I saw how hard Samantha worked to parent Lennon, to love her and provide for her.

My fist clenched on the wheel, a streak of anger I didn't know I had in me overwhelming my system. If that guy would have taken one step out of bounds today, I would have clocked him in the nose.

I give her some space, letting her think during the rest of the ride, until we reach the door to my apartment. As soon as we walk inside, I wrap her in a hug, needing to feel her just as much as I want to comfort her.

"Don't worry about it, babe. Give it some time. He may be serious in wanting to be a more active part of her life ... which is a good thing. Or this may be a fluke, and he could be gone tomorrow."

I bend down, letting my lips take hers, trying to smooth away the stress I know is vibrating through her.

She breaks off, walking across my apartment. "Don't worry about it? I can't just not worry about it, Jake ... this is my child we're talking about."

I hear the annoyance in her tone. "That's not what I meant—
"

"I get that you don't have to bother yourself with such serious matters, but this could have some disastrous complications on my life."

I can feel the wheels of anxiety start to turn in her head, and all I want is to wrap her up in my arms. But instead, I try to reason with her, and let the backhanded comment about me slide off my shoulders. "I know that, babe, but you can't go into panic mode just yet. Let's take a breath, calm down."

She throws her hands up. "Calm down?! Did anyone ever tell

you not to tell a woman to calm down? This is my daughter, Jake! He's threatening to take her away from me, and you're advice is to breathe! Like some horrible fortune cookie or something."

"He threatened to take her?" The sentence blindsides me.

Samantha stomps across the apartment, her coat and purse still on. "Yes! He said that because I was gallivanting around with you, that he was going to go to the courts about custody."

The accusation smacks me in the face, and guilt roils in my gut. So I put her in this position. "He can't do that, can he?"

She faces me, the look on her face saying that I must be the dumbest son-of-a-bitch alive. "Of course he can. We never had a formal arrangement, had always said we'd work it out between us. But now ... now he could make this a legal battle. I don't know what the hell I was thinking, putting her security in jeopardy like that."

"Putting her security in jeopardy because of what ... me? That's bullshit and you know it, Samantha. I love that little girl." Now my temper came out to play, reacting like gunpowder to a match as she lit me up.

Her eyes fill with rage, and I know we are only lashing out because of Derek showing up, but we can't stop.

"Oh come off it, Jake ... you told me that you didn't want to be that girl's father. You don't want the responsibility of being in her life, in our lives! I knew from the start that you were just here for a good time, and I should have stuck to that notion."

My heart burns with fury, and for the first time I know what it feels like when they say love hurts. "That's fucking bullshit, Samantha! I'm here, I've been here. Sure, at the beginning I was a little spooked, but I love you. And I love Lennon. Don't take this out on me, when all I'm doing is supporting you and trying to help you in any way I can to get through this. Don't push me away, I love you."

I'm saddened that I'm saying those words out of anger. Before now, they've only been said in perfect situations. In the middle of vineyards, in front of the Lincoln Memorial with the sun setting. But life wasn't perfect, and God knew we were far from it. This was real. This was the real shit that Samantha was always talking about.

My confession seemed to make her stutter, her hand fisted in her hair as tears blinked in her eyes.

"I should go, I need to be alone tonight. To clear my head. If Derek is serious about this, then we should spend some time apart anyway."

She crosses the room, and I reach out, my arm catching the softness of her jacket. "Don't do this, you don't mean it. I'm going to be here whether he takes things to court, whether you want to run away from me, whether you think that we can't get through it together. Don't go."

Her brown eyes shift, her lip trembles. "I have to go."

I release her arm, knowing that there is no getting past the blowup tonight. She's wounded and scared, and I know in this moment that she's not going to listen to reason. She went from zero to sixty in under a minute flat, and I couldn't do anything to stop it. She'd probably been brewing since the park, since her and Derek sat on that bench and talked. There was no way I could have prevented this.

"I love you, Samantha. And I'll be right here when you realize that."

All I get is the slamming of my apartment door.

28

JAKE

I gave her four hours.

Four hours of pacing my apartment, almost ripping my hair out. I even contemplated cleaning the oven, something Alice always tells me makes her feel better, before I decide to go over there.

I love her, dammit, and I love Lennon. I'm not going to be an outsider during this, and if I have to give Derek a piece of my own mind, I surely will. She may not want to be smothered right now, but too bad. That's what I was here for, to be her punching bag and pillow to cry on.

Walking into her building, I wave to Jerry at the front desk.

"Hey, Jake." He gives his usual salute, and I remind myself that he wasn't the guard on duty this afternoon when Derek had come in.

For that person would surely know something weird is going on. I send up a little thank you to the big man upstairs that Jerry didn't see the awkward family reunion just hours before, because he might have some questions before I was allowed up to see Samantha. Or worse, make a call up to her before letting me go up. She might say no, and surprise was the only thing working in my favor right now.

As I ride the elevator up, I think of everything we've been through thus far. That disastrous first date where I weaseled out of replacement-dad duty. One hot fucking night at the bar that ended up in my apartment. Jesus, thinking about Samantha naked under me for the first time almost distracts me from what I need to get done. Working hard to keep our relationship going, to even make it exist between our hectic schedules, her daughter, and both of our inabilities to fully commit. And then finally committing, giving in to the feelings and seeing where it went.

Which brought us here, to me standing in her elevator like some white knight climbing the castle to save her from the dragon. Only we were living in two thousand seventeen, and I wasn't climbing a rope made of her hair, and the dragon was a metaphor for her own heart standing in the way. Hell, I have been reading way too many fairy tales to Lennon.

The elevator dings as it hits Samantha's floor, and I take my keyring out of my pocket, flipping to her key. She'd given it to me two weeks ago, dropping it in my morning coffee cup like some kind of romantic comedy movie. I'd joked with her, making up nicknames for what the movie of us would be called. But deep down, the gesture wasn't lost on me. It was an advance of our relationship, and it meant she trusted me with her most precious belongings.

I don't knock, if she knew anything about me by now, she should know I was bound to come over here anyway. Unlocking the door, I walk in, the apartment quiet and calm without the little rugrat running around before bedtime. It ticked me off that Derek had shown up, a flickering candle of fury had been lit in the back of my mind since he'd walked across her lobby this morning. He had no claim to be a father anymore. Not when he had missed so much, for so long.

"Babe?" I call out quietly, not wanting to wake her if she fell asleep out of exhaustion.

"Why am I not surprised?" Her face is makeup free, and I notice my extra-large T-shirt hanging off of her as she walks into the kitchen.

I don't give her a minute to start the argument again. Instead, I cross the room, my body quickly finding hers, and sweep her up into my arms, covering her lips.

"Sto—" she protests, trying to turn her head.

The dominant in me comes out, forcing her mouth to mine. Samantha wants to put up her walls now, and I want to do nothing but smash them. I use my tongue to coax her aching heart to trust, my teeth to nibble at her stubborn pride. My mouth acts as my reasoning tool, talking to her mind and heart when I physically can't.

After thirty seconds of trying to push me away, Samantha melts into the kiss, sighing in a relieved way and letting me take control. I assault her mouth in a slow barrage of kisses, only pulling away when I feel that she won't fight me any longer.

"You don't get to walk away, okay? If you want to use me as a punching bag, do it. But you don't get to leave." I press my forehead against hers.

"Okay," she whispers, her fingers tangling in my shirt.

I move us to the small table in her kitchen, realizing neither of us has probably eaten since this morning.

"I'm sorry, baby ..." She chokes it out and then clears her throat. "I just ... what if he files? I can't lose her, Jake. I can't do the joint custody, shipping her back and forth. And maybe I could if I knew he was sincere, but this is Derek. God, I know I haven't talked about him much, but he doesn't care about her. That's a horrible thing to say about the father of my child, and I know deep down he loves her in some way, but he doesn't *care* about her. He doesn't want the responsibility. How could you not fucking want that?! Just look at her!"

Samantha buries her face in her hands, and I let her bang a fist on the table in frustration.

"If she were mine, I'd be calling her every single night to see how her day went. No, actually I wouldn't. I would fucking be here, move my life so that it could include that little girl. I'm furious he's here, you don't know how hard it was to keep my fists by my side while I watched him play with her in the park."

"I know that, you don't think I know that?" she whispers, and I can hear the tears in her throat. "Seeing him again ... it isn't pleasant, babe. I don't feel the way I once did, but it doesn't mean there aren't feelings of regret or resentment there. When I was with him ... I thought I was defective. Like if he hadn't asked me to marry him in all of those years, there was something wrong with me. With her. That we weren't enough, that we couldn't be loved enough to warrant that kind of commitment."

That flicker of fury turns into a burning torch, and I want to pick up my pitchfork and go hunt the bastard.

Grasping the sides of her face, I make those chocolate eyes look straight into mine. "And you know that's not fucking true. I love you, and I love Lennon. He's an idiot if he can't see how good he had it. How good he still does, because clearly that little girl holds no grudge against him."

"What am I going to do if he takes this to court?" Her eyes plead with me for an answer.

"*We* are going to fight. Hell, I'll fight him colosseum style to the death. He's not going to win, babe. Honestly, the guy has shown no balls thus far. He's probably bluffing because he's feeling neglected and wants attention from you. Because you gave it to him for so long without him having to give any back. And that's not on you at all, I'm just saying that it's his MO."

She nodded, still not looking convinced.

I scoot my chair so that her legs are positioned between mine, and hold her hands. "I promise you, everything is going to work out. And have I ever lied to you?"

Those gorgeous cherry lips give me a half-smile. "One time you said that you liked my chicken Alfredo, but two weeks later when we were out to dinner you said you hated Alfredo sauce."

I tickle her hip lightly. "That was a white lie. And if I'd eat Alfredo for you, *bleh*, you must know that I love you?"

"I guess it must be true." Her hand traces the hair on my arm.

"Now that that's settled, I'm going to feed you. Not Alfredo sauce, because I'm not sure why the people of Earth love that cheesy unflavored mess so much, but I'll whip something up."

I go to stand, but Samantha's hand catches my belt. "What if I'm not hungry?"

I hold onto Jake's belt, my tired mind and body reinvigorating in the way only make up sex can influence a person.

"I'm a chef, babe. I know how to do two things. Feed and eat. So which one do you want to choose?" His green eyes light with a challenge and I'm instantly damp.

Half the reason I'm head over heels for this man is because his sexual appetite hits all of the courses on my menu. He's a real artist in the bedroom, and I'm the lucky recipient of his work.

"Eat. Please."

But I don't mean him eating me. Before he can move, I unbuckle his pants, pulling his cock out in one swift motion. He's hard, thick and veiny already … jutting out parallel to my mouth.

"Samantha …" I think it's a question or a prayer.

He fought for me, didn't let me run when I so desperately wanted to sprint from connection or any hint of complication. And I wanted to praise him for it in the best way I knew how.

I scoot forward on my chair, making sure to lock eyes with

him as I move my lips toward his leaking head. The minute I make contact, one small touch to the crown of him, Jake hisses. He's salty and musky, an erotic scent that fills my head as I test out my motions. I slide my mouth down over him, taking him as far as I can and wetting his stiff pole. I leave my hands behind my back, knowing this drives him crazy when I only use my mouth.

"Fuck yes, I love it when you slide all the way down." He fists a hand in my hair, not forcing, but not letting me up all the way either.

It's funny, normally I would have said I didn't want a man who was controlling during sex. I like to think of myself as an independent woman, and therefore have a mental block when it comes to submitting. But with Jake ... it's so exciting. There is no other word for it. It sends a thrill up my spine every time he demands a little too much. Every time he binds my wrists or holds my head down while I suck him. We don't use whips, chains or any other toys besides our bodies really ... but something about the way he commands just does it for me. Gives me the little extra thrill I need to mark all my checkboxes.

I'm licking his tip when I'm suddenly hoisted up by the shoulders and begin to move.

Except, instead of picking me up so we're face to face so I can kiss him, Jake has me thrown over his shoulder.

I can't help but giggle. "What're you doing?"

"You deserve a little punishment." He swats my ass harmlessly. "You started a fight with me earlier, and then you almost sucked me off until I came in your mouth. You know better ... I always want to finish inside of you."

See, that right there. Filthy mouth, topped off with that sweet dimple. It mixes a woman up in the head, and apparently, my lady parts craved that.

He threw me down on the bed ... which had really become

our bed. Jake's support foam pillow had taken up residence on the left side. With no trouble at all, he lifts his shirt off my body, unveiling my nudity beneath. We both suck in a breath; me as my nipples hit the air, budding, and him at the sight of me. My inner ego preens ... Jake always seems to make me feel undeniably beautiful whenever he looks at me.

"I can think of no better way to make up." He shrugs out of his shoes and jeans, leaving his T-shirt on.

And then he's pulling me to the end of the bed, no warm up, no foreplay. I part my legs for him, my ass hanging over the edge as he holds both legs just below my knees. Standing on the floor like that, he towers over me, his dick positioned at my entrance. I squirm, knowing how he'll deliciously impale me. This is exactly what I need.

"I love you," I breathe as he slides into me, thick and pulsing as he pushes in to the hilt.

Jake bends over me, hooking my legs around his waist to free his hands and plant them on either side of my face. He looks like a track runner about to win a race, his jaw tight and his green pools intense as they stare down at me. There is something even sexier about making love with clothes on sometimes ... the pulling of material, the less is more effect.

"You. Are. So. Perfect." Jake hits on the words every time he slides back into me, maintaining a slow but hard pace.

My toes curl, my thighs shaking as they grip the muscles at his waist. Goose bumps move across every inch of my skin as I get closer to orgasm, the climax coming on like a fever. This time feels different, there are more emotions floating around us. After our fight, it's a cathartic kind of sex, a rededicating of ourselves to each other.

It doesn't take long for all of my senses to act as one. My eyes seeing his body move, feeling him pleasure me. The scent of him, manly and in control, filling my nose. My teeth biting into my lips, almost drawing blood at how much I need to explode. Every groan and growl registering in my ears, heightening my own arousal.

"I'm going to come." I don't know if I say it as a warning, but I find myself nodding, everything inside of me saying *yes*.

"Come for me, baby." Jake thrusts in farther, finding nerves and spots that I didn't even know existed.

I focus on his eyes, my vision going white around everything but ferocious, magnetic green orbs.

"Yes, Samantha. Yes, baby ..." His fingers dig into my hips as I let go, and somewhere my conscious brain registers that he's unraveling too.

The room is filled with nothing but our sounds of release, guttural calls of pleasure piercing the silence. I let it wash over me, let Jake act like a drug that takes away the worry and pain of the day.

And when he pulls out of me, crawling up the bed to bury his face in my neck, I breathe him in. The future may be unclear and full of scary uncertainty, but at least I have this man beside me.

I know now that to try and run, to try and preserve myself, is one level of foolish I won't be again.

A fter Derek leaves to go back to Seattle, with another tension filled discussion in the lobby of his hotel, time seems to drag and fly at the same time.

September flies by, and October arrives with its annual Halloween costume debacle. Every year, Lennon tells me she wants to be one thing, so I buy the costume, only to be told three days before the spookiest night of the year that she wants to be something else. The month also brings with it more stress at work, preparing the colder climate national parks for the change in the seasons. Nights are sometimes late, and early bird me also likes to start on Christmas shopping before the malls and stores get crazy in November and December.

My autumn is also filled with Jake, who practically lives with us now. His toothbrush is in the bathroom, his sneakers and socks are tossed by the front door. He picks up takeout on his way home, sometimes surprising Lennon with his newest flavor of ice cream as a treat. Once a weekend, he'll take her by the construction on the new storefront, or for a ride around one of the neighborhoods in the truck. We're better than ever, even if we do have our fights about leaving dishes in the sink or throwing the comforter off the bed in the middle of the night.

In some ways, the clock doesn't seem to stand still. But in others, I'm just waiting for the axe to fall. I've only received the occasional call from Derek since he left a month ago, and he usually asks me straight away to put his daughter on the phone. He never mentions filing for custody or what he has up his sleeve; he just leaves me dangling, with little passive aggressive sharks biting into my brain with doubt-filled teeth. Not knowing is the worst part. Sometimes I'll wake up in the middle of the night in a cold sweat, wondering if I should be protecting myself. Wondering if I should get a lawyer or ... do something.

But he still could be bluffing, and if I make a move, there is no telling what damage I could do before he has a chance to back down. I feel like I'm navigating hot lava, trying very hard to stay still or move only when absolutely necessary.

Trying to push it out of my head, I focus on the Internet browser in front of me. Princess birthday invitations light up the screen, and I add them to my cart. Next month is Lennon's fourth birthday, and we're doing a birthday party at the local trampoline place. She won't stop babbling about it, and it's over a month away ... I find it hilariously cute.

"Does she have her costume ready?" Jake walks in the door, his face resembling a hyped up puppy.

"I thought we weren't leaving for another hour ..." He breezes by me, planting a kiss on my cheek as he searches for Lennon.

"I'm ready!" She pops out of her room in her costume, and I burst into laughter.

For some reason, she insisted on being that hippo from the Cincinnati Zoo. She loved Fiona, the animal Instagram star, and so we'd pieced together her costume with gray and purple sweats. I'd found hippo ears and a nose online, and added some lettuce leaves on her sleeves because we knew that Fiona liked to eat those. She looked adorable, and I loved her creativity.

It was a rather easy costume, and I thanked my lucky stars that she hadn't wanted to be something that involved sewing fifty two pieces together.

"Look at you! Cuter than any baby hippo I've ever seen." He scoops her up, making what I can only assume are his best hippo noises. "You ready to go Truck or Treating?"

"YEAH!" She pumps a fist in the air.

"Mommy, you have to get in your costume." Jake smiles at me, mischief in his eye.

I roll my eyes, annoyed that I even have to dress up. "You know, last year all I did was trail behind her and hold the pillow sack. Can't I just do that again?"

"No!" They both say in unison.

Twenty minutes later and we're all in our costumes, headed down to the car.

"I don't understand why I had to be the giraffe," I mutter, annoyed.

"Because the skin tight spotted suit so wasn't going to fit me. Plus, your ass looks better," Jake whispers as he closes Lennon's door.

I swear to God, he only ordered this because I look like Catwoman ... except, well, I'm a giraffe. He's in a penguin costume, claiming he had to be a penguin to peddle ice cream around on Halloween.

Or correction, the day before Halloween. Since some of the neighborhoods around DC weren't particularly kid friendly, or safe, Jake and some of his food truck friends had set this up two years ago. Truck or Treating happened the day before Halloween, in a local park where they all got permits to park. They sold their products, but also had huge tubs of candy out front for the kids to go truck to truck. And twenty percent of the proceeds were donated to charities to help at-risk youth around the city.

If I didn't already think he was a superhero, Jake just grew ten feet in my eyes.

Plus, it would give Lennon somewhere to experience a real Halloween in DC. She probably didn't remember it, but back in Seattle, we lived in a townhouse bordered by a bunch of other young families with children. In our apartment, she really wouldn't get that same experience. I was thinking about taking her to Mom's neighborhood, but this would be a great bonus.

"Oh my God, there are so many people here." I couldn't help being surprised as we parked and got out of the car.

Parked along the sidewalk and overlooking a grassy park were over a dozen food trucks, people lined up at them to buy some grub. Children in costumes of all sorts ran through the park, yelling and laughing and trading candy.

"I told you, it's a big deal." Jake holds my hand as he hoists Lennon up on his waist. "I'm *kind of* a regular charity superstar."

"Can it, Bono." I walk to Cones & Corks and see Alice already scooping.

"'Sup, guys?!" Jake's business partner waves at us, and Lennon shrinks back a bit.

To be honest, I think Lennon forgets who Alice is because she is constantly changing the color of her hair. Today it is bright neon yellow, and I wonder where she even found a dye that color. She's dressed like some kind of zombie rockstar, and I'm afraid she might be scaring the children but don't say anything because I'm cautious of what she'll say in front of my daughter. While I like Alice, and I know she means well, she isn't exactly kid friendly.

"You think maybe you could have gone with a little bit more G-rated of a costume?" Jake laughs.

Well, at least he isn't afraid to say something.

"Lennon, never work for someone else. The boss is always ragging on your balls." She shoots my daughter a silly look, which makes her laugh.

"Alice, really? Language." I chuckle, but can't be too mad. She's kind of lovably annoying.

"Great turnout, we've sold out of two flavors already. Go on out, I'll hold down the fort. Lennon, I expect your pillowcase to be full of candy when you get back, so get to it. Score some Twizzlers for Aunt Alice." Alice nods at her and salutes, going to help the next customer.

We went back out, walking to the first truck. Lennon ran a little ahead of us, familiar with some of the truck owners now that Jake had been taking her around some of the festivals recently.

"You look incredible. This penguin definitely wants to mate with you." He leaned into me, doing some kind of weird sniffing, animal thing.

I lean into him, unable to stop from smiling even if I was annoyed that he made me wear this costume. "That would be a pretty weird looking baby."

"But it would be fun trying to make it. We would make some pretty adorable babies."

He says it so off the cuff that it catches me by surprise. Over the course of the past few months, we've become more intimate and closer then I guess I realized. Jake has become one of the people I turn to most in my life, he's practically living in our apartment, we don't do anything where he isn't involved. He's becoming closer to Lennon, and now I guess we were talking about babies?

Fuck. Our babies would be *so* adorable.

I never really thought about having more kids. Sure, maybe when Derek and I were still together and Lennon was one or so, it was a pipe dream that our family would grow. But when things began to get tough, I kind of put those thoughts out of my mind.

Having a family with Jake. It was an idea I hadn't really considered before, as we had said we were going slow at the very beginning. Since then, there hadn't really been a conversation about where this was going or how serious it was, it just kind of progressed through those steps and we'd become inseparable.

I realize I've been silent for a few seconds, and Jake is looking at me with a look that says, "maybe I shouldn't have said that."

"We would ... so long as they have your dimples." My grin is far off, thinking about what little Jake/Samantha kids would look like.

"And your eyes." His look into said eyes is deeper than the joking atmosphere we'd been teasing in before.

Sometimes, I forgot how young I still was, because as a single mom, I didn't much feel like it. But clearly, my boyfriend was thinking about things beyond right now. He was considering a future, a life with me. And maybe it wasn't such a pipe dream to think about what that could be.

31

JAKE

"We are going to get so much foot traffic."

Alice rubs her hands together, examining the thousand square foot store front that was currently under construction.

"That's what I'm hoping for." I nod, looking around the space and seeing all of the vision boards I'd designed with the interior decorators coming to life.

It turned out, pairing with the Foodie Conglomerate hadn't been the wish and a prayer I'd been doubtful to bank on. They were the real deal, bringing us in for a meeting a month ago and basically moving lightyears since then. They'd believed in us, listened to our ideas for expansion and brought in the best people to help us. With their help, we'd scouted locations around the nation's capital until we found the perfect space right on the Georgetown strip. I'd sat down with the trendiest designers, who were perceptive to my idea of both a bar and an ice cream shop. They'd worked to secure us permits, a crew, and anything else we needed.

And now here we stood, in the half-finished brainchild we'd always dreamt about. The walls were painted a creamy beige, the color of coffee with almond milk. Along one wall stood a long, weathered white counter with a wood top. It held the cash register, and empty stainless steel pits, twelve of them total. They were individual freezer systems, and I'd found the idea in an industry magazine. Instead of having the typical ugly white bubble case to hold our ice cream, we were going to showcase the flavors like they deserved to be. The wall behind it was blank, but Alice had a local artist friend who was going to come in and do a word art mural for us. I'd seen the mockups, and was so excited about it that I almost got a boner thinking about how awesome it was going to look.

The bar was along the other wall. A dark, grainy wood with copper stools seated neatly in front of it, the construction on my favorite part of the restaurant was finally complete. And that part ... it took my breath away. An entire wall, top to bottom, of criss-crossing wood beams that created a giant wine rack. It was better than a blow job.

Okay, maybe not a blowjob. But it was close.

"Do you think we'll scare away some of the families with the bar aspect?" Alice rubs her hand across her chin.

"Getting spooked? I thought you had faith in our vision," I tease her. "No, we've run the numbers with the business guys at Foodie; they think it will only increase sales. It attracts the college crowd, as well as younger parents who want a more hip family place to bring their kids to. This allows them to not only get a sweet treat for little Timmy or Susie, but also let their hair down a bit with a glass of Pinot Grigio."

"Look at the sales guy over here talking figures and estimates. Who are you?" Alice hoists herself onto one of the mismatched stools standing by the bar.

"I did graduate with a business degree, smart-ass."

Jana came up from the back, her eyes wide. "Can't believe

that kitchen. You are going to make some kickass dessert in that kitchen."

She fist bumped me, which made me grin. Usually, she was a little more reserved, but I think we were wearing off on her.

"Should we do a taste test? I think it's only fitting that the three of us pick the first wines we'll feature." Alice pulls a crate up, one that I didn't know she'd been hiding there, from behind the bar.

"Technically, we don't have a liquor license yet ..." I bit my lip.

"Stop being a pussy." Jana slaps my shoulder.

Alice and I bust out laughing, because we've definitely corrupted her over the years.

We all pull up a stool, the shapes and sizes unmatching because we're still trying to decide on decor. As Alice pours us each a taste of the four bottles she brought into red Solo cups, I can't help but sit back and revel in it.

"Who would have ever thought we'd make it here?"

Cones & Corks had been a half-assed business scheme when it had popped into my head. I'd rented the first truck, fixed it up with the help of Bryan ... and man had I bought him a lot of alcohol to cover the costs of labor. That truck had been my baby, I'd slept in it some nights. I would drive that thing for hours, doing a secret little shimmy of my hips whenever I made a sale to some kid in a neighborhood, or a woman looking for an after work pick me up. I'd had to give a quarter of my profits back to the rental company, and covering overhead costs of making the ice cream in my own apartment kitchen had nearly bankrupt me. But I'd believed in it. Sure, I didn't quite know that we'd be here three years later, but I had never stopped.

"I did." Jana speaks after we all taste the first wine, her head bobbing that the grape was good. "When I joined y'all, I had this feeling that I was coming on to something bigger than just that little office space we used to have."

"That's so sweet." Alice gave her a sugary smile and we all laughed because it was such a weird expression on her face.

"I think that in honor of us, Jake should create flavors with our name for the opening. I vote for Jana Jamocha!"

Alice grumbles. "Not named-after flavors again."

Starting on my third glass, a deliciously dry red, I nod in agreement. "It's a must. I'll make you some sour apple flavor, Alice, to match your soul."

"Do you think we'll make it a year?" It's the first time I think I've ever heard a niggle of doubt in Alice's voice.

"I have to believe we will. Otherwise, we're shooting ourselves in the foot before we even open."

There was a shadowy omen, or curse, that most restaurants sunk within a year. And while it was always a thought in the back of my mind, I just kept moving. I would sweat and bleed for this place, so that it wouldn't fail.

"If he says so, then I'll take it as sermon. Oh wise one." Alice raises her hands and bows to me.

"In a year from now, let's do a shot of Jamo at this very bar." I finish my last Solo cup and sit back.

"I thought we didn't really do liquor." Alice makes a good point.

"We're wine snobs, yes ... but for celebration I think we can make an exception."

We all nod quietly, and I pray like hell to whatever God listens to my unrepentant ass that we strike gold.

32

Mom stands over the stove, mixing a giant pot of tomato sauce.

"I'm not sure why you're making enough food to feed the state of Texas. It's just the three of us tonight."

Jake was at the restaurant again, it being crunch time and all before the soft opening in a month or so. They were putting the final touches on everything, cleaning down the place, beginning to mix flavors in the new kitchen in the back. It was actually really cute to see how excited he was about it, and I beamed with pride whenever we were out and someone asked him how it was going. You could hear the tangible joy in his voice, and I for one was thrilled to have a bar I could hang out in that I could also bring my kid to.

"I don't know ... I'm still used to your brother being here. Even though, I know, he's been overseas for two years. But once you're a mother, some behaviors you just can't go back on. Plus, I can send a bunch home with you for Jake. He'll always eat it."

That was true. Since he'd basically moved himself in, our food seemed to disappear in a matter of days.

"How are things going by the way?" If that wasn't a fishing expedition, I wasn't sure what was.

She's lucky I'm in the mood to share. "Things are great, actually. He's ... well, amazing."

"I should have thought to fix you two up a while ago. In fact, I may have mentioned when he was on route in the truck one time that I had a daughter. Funny how fate works."

Yes, it was. "He's great with her, too."

Mom smiles, looking back. "That's a good man right there, Samantha Jean. Don't let him go."

I wasn't planning to. "Mom, did you ever want to date after Dad?"

The spoon she's stirring in the pot slows, and I know she's thinking about how to phrase her thoughts.

"I tried, honestly I did. But ... your father was my best friend. Sure, I've thought about it as I grow older, having a companion might be nice after all. But ... I'm not sure why, I just can't seem to invest in anyone I meet. Your father might be gone for a long while now, but I still think about him every day. Maybe that's what happens, you find the person you're meant to be with and you have as much time as this earth grants you and then that's it. I feel like ... if I tried to make that happen with anyone else, I'd just be lying to myself."

I frown. "That makes me sad for you, Mom."

She smiles complacently. "Don't be. I had a wonderful marriage for many years. And now I have you back, and I have my granddaughter. I have my hobbies and my work, I'm perfectly happy. Sometimes, you get what you need, but not all at once. That's life."

Her easy shrug as she goes back to making dinner, dumping the pasta and stirring in homemade meatballs to the sauce, gives me some ... closure. For a while after I had decided to move home, those transitional months in Seattle where Derek and I weren't really together but I had some hope, I was devastated. Devastated that I couldn't make it work with the father of my child. Horrified that I'd become just another single mother statistic, that I hadn't done things in the "right societal order," so someone was punishing me. Why couldn't I have the baby and the love and marriage?

But Mom's words strike a chord. That's life. I have my beautiful daughter. I struggled with becoming independent, but I did it. And now I had found that love I'd been looking for. It may have come together in a patchwork sewn together in the wrong order, but at the end of the day, I had one complete quilt.

"Let's eat. You're getting too skinny." Such a mom thing to say.

Looking into the living room, I see Lennon asleep on the couch. She had a fun filled day with Grandma, and I decide to let her sleep, knowing that could make for a disaster tonight. But it was the weekend and I was okay with being a bad mom right now. My appetite didn't want to wait, and I chose myself in the tiniest of ways.

Right as we were about to sit down, the table set with steaming bowls of comfort, my phone dinged.

"Turn it off," Mom scolds me, still not allowing cell phones at her table.

"One second, Mother." I can't help but sound like myself at sixteen.

Derek: *Got job offer in Argentina. Will be flying out in an hour. Tell Lennon I love her and will try and call when I get settled.*

"Are you fucking kidding me?" I stare at my phone, dumbfounded.

"You're lucky she's asleep." Mom pointed to Lennon napping on the couch, a cartoon playing on the TV in the background.

I keep staring at the illuminated screen, relief and fury coursing through my body like antidotes to one and other.

"He left." I can't seem to form more words than that.

"Jake?! Oh, honey—"

I cut her off, because she'll just go into some speech about how strong I am. "No, Derek. He's moving. To Argentina."

She crumples up the napkin in her fist. "That bastard."

There is nothing I can think of to type back. I want to tell him to go fuck himself. I want to wish him well. I both want him out of our lives and in hers as well. I feel guilt that I'm glad he's moving to a country where he will no longer be a factor in my parenting of Lennon. That this most likely means he's moved on from trying to be a father, and won't file for custody. But it's also euphoric, not having that worry sitting on my shoulders anymore. I've won the parent contest, and that little devil sits on my shoulder grinning.

But at the same time, my heart breaks for Lennon. How dare he abandon that beautiful little girl? With her amazing spirit, and sassy personality ... as Jake had said, how could he not want to be here for every moment of this? It was gut wrenching.

"Do I ask if he is coming back? Do I mention anything about what he said about court? I don't even know what to say right now." Tears spring into the corners of my eyes, and I don't know if they're from relief or upset.

She gets out of her chair, moving to rub my shoulders and kiss the side of my forehead. "Take this is a blessing in disguise. That man never wanted to be that little girl's father, not what it truly means to be that anyhow. He's leaving. This is his way of skating away untouched, his easy out. Let him have it. You and she are both better off without him, and you get to keep her right where you want her. Tell him good riddance, and if anything this is just fodder for you to hit him where it hurts if he ever did come back and try anything."

I nodded, knowing she's right. But I need just a little bite of revenge. I needed to stick it to Derek, get some closure. I'd been so tight-lipped when it came to him, tried to take the high road. For once, I was going a little low.

So I picked up the phone and called him. I wasn't doing this over text like his coward ass.

He picks up on the third ring. "Hey, Sammy."

I don't even say hello. "Were you going to say goodbye to your daughter, or just leave like usual?"

So yeah, I was a little more bitter than I thought I was before I'd gotten on the phone.

"Don't be like that ... this is a huge deal for me. You know I love her."

"Actually, Derek, I'm beginning to think that I don't. Were you even going to speak to her? Explain to her why you weren't going to be here for her, again? Especially after what you pulled when you showed up here?"

There is a pause. "Yeah about that, I think I got ahead of myself, Sammy. I wasn't going to really take you to court."

I have to bite my fist before answering. "No, because that would require follow through. Have a nice trip, or stay, or whatever you're doing. But please, don't contact your daughter if you aren't serious about being in her life. It will be painful for her at first, but not as painful as a father who only loves her when he remembers to."

More silence. And then he clears his throat. "Understood. You're right, Sammy."

Jesus. I bite back an expletive. I hadn't really expected to lay down that ultimatum, but part of me hoped he'd fight for her. That he would get angry or yell at me for saying that. Complacency and unaffected defeat were even worse. Because it meant he truly did not care.

"Goodbye, Derek." I click off before he can say anything else.

Mom just hugs her arms around my shoulders, knowing that there didn't need to be any words.

It felt like the end of an era. What I hadn't realized when I'd moved back to Washington DC was that I still had that resentment of Derek eating away inside of me. I'd needed to tell him the business, to be a badass mom and serve him up some truth.

And now I needed to go home with my girl, and vent to the one man who would reassure both of us that there were still males of this species worthy of being with.

33

SAMANTHA

That night, Jake held me as I silently sobbed into his shoulder so that Lennon couldn't hear in the next room.

"He didn't even fight for her. How do you not fight for her?!" I wailed, my melodrama reaching new heights.

He rubbed my shoulder and my back, kissing my forehead as I buried my face in his bare chest. "Because he's a complete ass wipe who should burn in hell if you ask me. Hey, beautiful ... look at me."

I look up, slightly aware that there has got to be snot and tears running down my face.

"You don't need him. We don't need him. I told you before, I'm going to be in that girl's life forever. You're not getting rid of me, baby. And I'm not asking, I'm telling ... I plan to be the best kind of father you'll let me be to Lennon."

I try to speak, but gurgle. "Can I ... can I have a tissue?"

He chuckles, his eyes so kind and loving. "Of course."

Leaning over, he grabs a few from the box off the nightstand and hands them to me, helping to wipe my face too.

"If I can clean your boogers, I must really love you, huh?" Jake looks me in the eye.

"I suppose you do. You know ... it's a big commitment—"

Jake puts a finger to my lips, stopping my mouth from moving. "Stop it. We're not going over this again. You're going to warn me about some bullshit that you worry I won't be able to handle, and I try to talk you into it. I'm here. I love you. I love her. It's simple."

His quirked eyebrow makes a small smile spread across my face. "And you'll love me even though I'm an ugly crier?"

"Your crying face is more beautiful than any I've ever seen. Although Lennon rivals you. When she's in temper tantrum mode ... hell, that is a sight to behold."

We both laugh, careful not to be too loud as we don't want to wake her in the next room.

"Do you remember that first date? God, she'd gone nuclear in that aquarium." I giggled.

"Do I remember?! I thought you'd never want to see me again. 'God, that guy who couldn't handle the tears of a three-year-old.' You probably thought I was some wimp."

"Actually, I thought you were quite cute trying as hard as you did to include my kid. But be honest, that was just a move to get in my pants, right? No sane man would suggest a woman bringing her daughter on the first date if they weren't trying to fuck."

Jake shrugs. "So what if I was? It worked didn't it."

I trace the lines in his abs, still dreamy-eyed when it came to his body. "Eventually, yes."

"What do you think it would have been like if I'd had the guts to ask you out in college like I'd wanted to?"

I wonder, and laugh. "We probably would have gone on some lousy date to the dining hall, you would have drunk texted me, we'd have had terrible, amateur college sex and then never called each other again."

He puts a hand over his heart. "Ouch ... but you're probably right. I like how it happened better anyway. You know, the dashing DC entrepreneur swoops in to sweep the single mom off of her feet. Wooing her with his good lucks, dimple and charm until she had no choice but to fall in love with him."

I bite his shoulder in a playful tease. "Oh lord, you really are so humble, aren't you?"

"I love you, Samantha."

Those words still took my breath away, as if it was the first time I was hearing them.

"I love you, too. Can you do one more thing for me tonight?" I bat my eyelashes.

"Anything."

"Do your job and go scoop me some ice cream. Nothing tops off a cure of the cries like ice cream."

Jake tapped his hands on the steering wheel like he was a five-year-old waiting for Christmas morning.

"You know that I have little to no restaurant expertise. You could take me to Taco Bell and impress me, so stop worrying."

I rub his thigh over the passenger console, letting my hand linger. Maybe if his brain registers I'm getting close to his dick, he'll stop being a basket case. *Men.*

It was our once a week standing lunch date, and instead of eating takeout in my office or his, I'd insisted he take me to the restaurant. I'd been waiting patiently to see it, and he's been delaying until every single detail is perfect. They're due to open in just three short days, and I basically all but grabbed him by his balls, demanding to be given a tour.

He pulls the truck up out front, paralleling into an empty spot. The sign is now over the door, which it wasn't when I'd driven by for a peek inside before. It was the typical Cones & Corks logo, neat script and a wine cork making up the *k*, but it looked so different over a storefront as opposed to on the side of a truck.

"Fancyyy, Brady. Very *fancy*." I pat his shoulder like we're teammates or something.

"Wait until you see the inside." He hops out, and I swear he skips to unlock the door.

Damn, that ass is amazing. Sometimes when he's sleeping, I just stare at it. Which sounds creepy, but it's a work of art that needs to be worshipped.

The door opens and I smell the scent of ... new. Just the smell of freshness, or cleaning products, that lets you know that this place hasn't been tarnished yet.

"Holy shit." I couldn't help the words.

It was ... freaking gorgeous. One side was all white tile and stainless steel, bright colors detailing the flavors on the wall and high-top tables of dark wood. And then on the other wall, a dark oak bar, with a wine rack spreading from floor to ceiling behind it. The whole store has a relaxed but spunky vibe; it's going to make a wonderful spot for families and young singles alike.

"This is perfect. Jake ... it's going to dominate."

He stands behind me, fist to his mouth. "You like it?"

"I love it. It's going to be perfect ... great for families but also singles. The bar and ice cream parlor combo was a fantastic idea, and seriously? The little trucks over there. Oh my God!"

I made a whiny girl noise over the adorable model trucks lining the top of the ice cream barrels. They were tiny models of the Cones & Corks trucks, one positioned over each flavor.

"We had a local metal artist make those ... thought it would be a nice touch."

"They're adorable. You better get one for Lennon though, because she's going to whine until she gets one."

"Noted. You really like it?" He looks so nervous, it's so un-Jake-like.

I walk to him, pressing my body against his and looking up, watching his jaw spread into a small smile.

"As usual, everything you touch turns to gold. It's beyond, Jake ... more than I had imagined, honestly. Take a minute to pat yourself on the back, you earned it."

I knew, from our time visiting his family in Buffalo, that while he might look confident on the outside, he was waiting every other second for the other shoe to drop. He didn't think he was worthy, even after he'd busted his ass for years to make his business. When you're conditioned to think a certain way about yourself, you start to believe it.

"Now give me the rest of the tour so we can eat lunch. I look forward to my midday dates with my man."

Pressing up on my toes, I make him kiss me. Our lips fuse for a steamy couple of seconds before I pull back, swatting his butt.

Jake gives me the dimple, and then takes my hand, showing me features around the room like the milkshake machine, double sinks, and other kitchen gadgets that mean nothing to me but make his eyes light up.

He then leads me to the back, past a small staff room and bathroom.

"And this is the kitchen." Jake grabs my hips from behind, the old sparks lingering from our last foray into one of his test kitchens.

"Mmm, not the same counter as the one at your offices." I purposely back up into him, shimmying just the tiniest bit.

"Maybe we should test them out, see if they're up to par." His hands squeeze tighter.

Finally, I tip my head back, my body responding to his insinuation. "I think we might just have to do that. You know, for the sake of good business and all."

Water splashed onto the side of the cement pavilion, the waves from the Potomac River bouncing as the sun set below them.

I watched as the sun reflected off the glass windows of the Gaylord Hotel & Convention Center, the massive structure taking up an entire hill in Maryland's National Harbor.

"Okay, I have to admit it, maybe the East Coast isn't a dump." Lila, Samantha's best friend from Seattle, walks by popping a piece of donut in her mouth.

"Especially when we have our own London Eye. Er, well, I mean Maryland Eye. But still ... very international of us." Bryan winked at her while motioning to the large Ferris wheel like object.

"Your friend is a shameless flirt, huh? Does he realize I'm not going to sleep with him?"

I liked the blond spitfire already. She was feisty and raw in a way that Samantha was not, and I found that it brought out a side in my girlfriend that I rather liked. Plus, she was beating Bryan into his place.

"Sleep? Mommy sleeps with Jake." Lennon looks happy with herself after having announced this.

"Yes, she does, smarty pants." Lila kisses her cheeks where she rests in Samantha's arms, and I can't help but laugh.

I'd instantly liked Lila the moment we'd picked her up from Ronald Reagan. She'd skipped to the car, wrapped Samantha in a bear hug, thrown Lennon up in a launch of squeals, and then looked in the car at me and said, "Oh, Samantha, I'm proud of you, girlfriend. Nice catch."

And ever since Bryan had accidentally seen a picture of Lila on Samantha's phone, he'd instantly inserted himself into any activity we'd be doing while she was here. So, here the five of us were, shopping and munching at the National Harbor. So far, the girls had racked up some good purchases, gossiped, ignored us men, and eaten their weight in fast casual food.

It was nice to see Samantha in this atmosphere, surrounded by someone who she so clearly felt comfortable with. Rarely was she with friends, since she didn't have many left out here, and when we were together, it was usually just her, Lennon and me. I liked to listen to their little blips of conversation about this TV show or that person back in Seattle. About old memories or the new makeup they were trying. It gave me an insight into Samantha's head that I didn't normally get, and I stored away each nugget of knowledge like a gambling chip.

Of course, Lila's trip was double sided, but my girl didn't know that. She thought that our first meeting was in the airport, and physically it was. But virtually and over the phone ... we'd been corresponding for weeks now.

"So where should we go for dinner?" Samantha asks, looking a little tired.

I walk to her, lifting Lennon out of her arms and giving her a break. "Let's go to this Italian place just up ahead. Right on the water, we can look out. Plus, I know someone who wants some spaghetti and meatballs."

Lennon raises her hand, and both Samantha and Lila look at each other. Lila raises her eyebrows as if to say, "and he's good with the kid, too." Damn right, I am.

"Lila, if this coast isn't so bad, maybe you should stay awhile."

The blond makes a chuckling noise and sticks her finger in her mouth, fake-vomit style. "Bryan, this whole charade has got to stop. You're making a fool of yourself."

"That's only going to encourage him, Lila." I shake my head.

"Usually the ladies find me so charming." Bryan holds his hand over his heart.

"Oh God, did you just call us ladies? Yuck. And I guess some people would call you charming, but trust me ... I see enough idiot couples in the delivery room to know who is right for whom. Nothing like pushing a child out of your body to really test the strength of a relationship. And trust me, buddy, you don't have what it takes to handle me."

Oh shit. I think he might just fall in love with this one.

"What about us?" Samantha elbows her in jest.

"You and Jake? Yeah, you'd make it through. Knock my friend up, Jake, make some more cute babies like this one. You want a little brother, right Lennon?"

Lennon squeals. "I would like a baby sister named Princess Sofia, just like on Disney Channel!"

"You heard the girl." Lila winks at Samantha, who rolls her eyes and gives her the finger behind her daughter's back.

"Are we doing any more shopping before we eat?" Samantha looks longingly at some store called Alex & Ani.

"The men are hungry." I speak for Bryan and me because my stomach is growling. "This is my rare night away from the new place, and I want to spend it eating as much pasta as I can."

"And if I know you like I think I do, the way to your heart is most *definitely* through your stomach. So let's go eat." She wraps an arm around my waist and snuggles into my side.

Twenty minutes later, we're sitting at a table near the window, the waves dark under the night sky now. The Ferris wheel lights up the harbor, and the inside of the restaurant smells like garlic and cheese and fucking deliciousness.

"I bet you I can eat an entire plate of calamari." Lila rubs her stomach.

"Remember that one time we ordered one of every item on the Chinese menu and ate so much that we considered going to the hospital to have our stomach pumped?" Samantha laughs, rubbing her own stomach.

"I swore I could give us colonoscopies from the couch. Jesus, I don't think I've ever been so full."

As we ordered and talked and drank, a sense of calmness sets over me. After the debacle with my family, I'd tried to put it out of my mind. That I didn't really belong to anyone anymore.

But like I'd told Samantha before, family didn't have to be the people related to you by blood. They could be this motley crew. The beautiful single mother and her stubborn daughter. Her best friend with a quick wit and sarcastic attitude. Bryan, one of the closest people to me on this earth, even when he was drunk and rummaging through my cabinets or trying to convince me to let him crash on my couch when he lived next door.

I had Alice and Jana too, and more close friends down here in Maryland than I was able count on one hand.

Before I'd met these people, I'd been floating along without an anchor. I didn't have a dream or a purpose, and thought I was better off not having attachments. But I'd come to learn that strings weren't a burden, they were lifelines.

And knowing that, I enjoyed mounds of heaping family-style Italian food with some of my lifelines, until my stomach threatened to explode.

"**D**oes the person who helps pick out the ring get a present too? Because I see some earrings over there calling my name."

Lila stands next to me at the gleaming glass counter, the sales associate gone to fetch us some rings to look at. The jewelry store I picked is one in the middle of DC, an upscale, elegant place with sleek wood floors and rows and rows of priceless gems. They offered us champagne when we arrived, thinking we were a couple. Lila played it up for one second, but then cringed at trying on rings on her finger. Apparently, that was bad luck and she just couldn't do it to Samantha.

"I'll buy you a candy necklace." I smile, but bounce on the heels of my boat shoes as the anxiety courses through me.

"Normally, I'd ask if you were sure you wanted to do this. It's been only a short amount of time, and I don't want my Samantha or Lennon hurt. In fact, I'll skin you alive if you hurt either of them. *But,* I've seen how you are with them this weekend, and how they are with you. You're all really good together. I wouldn't be here helping if I didn't think so. So relax, Jake."

Lila lays a hand over mine, and I notice I'm leaving sweat marks on the glass. "I don't even know what to look for. Shit, should I have looked at one of her Pinterest boards or whatever?"

She slants her eyes at me. "Do you really think Samantha is the type of girl who has a Pinterest board, much less time for one?"

"Yeah, okay, you're right. I just ... I know she's probably thought about the perfect situation for all of this, and I want to do it right."

The sales woman is making her way back, but Lila scoffs. "I think Samantha used to dream about a wedding or fairy tale because she had the wrong guy next to her. It was nicer than facing the reality that she'd never have it with Derek. Harsh but true. With you, it won't matter if you pull that rock out of a paper lunch bag. She loves you in a way I've never seen her love before. You're the fairy tale, and the rest will just fall into place. Now let's look at some bling before you make me vomit on the sweet shit that's coming out of my mouth."

I can't help but laugh. "Deal. Just don't pick an ugly one, because I'll blame it on you if she hates it."

We look at the velvet jewelry cases set out before us, thousands of dollars sitting out on that counter. Square diamonds and round ones, yellow ones that I don't really like, bands with a lot of jewels and those with none. Gold and silver, thick and thin, ornate and simple.

"I've got to be honest, I'm completely lost." I fist a hand in my hair.

I feel like women should just constantly have a running Christmas list with anything they'll ever want to have on there. I'm not a chick, I don't read minds. One purse looks the same as another to me. And I definitely have no taste in jewelry.

"Okay, calm down. Gold is out, as are any other color diamonds but traditional. And she likes a round diamond, so that narrows us down." Lila shoos away some rings with her hand and the woman removes them from the bunch.

We're left with about eight, and my eyes automatically go to one in particular. It's unique, a little different from the others, and unlike any I've seen on another woman's finger. Not that I check much.

But it's solely Samantha. Unique, not round but not square ... never fitting a stereotype or role. It flourishes in a bunch of ordinary, and at the end of the day is always the brightest thing in the room. This ring is her, and I want to make her mine.

"That one. That's it."

SAMANTHA

J ake was wedged into Lennon's twin bed, her curled up into him was the cutest thing I'd ever seen.

"And then the princess let down her hair, and he climbed right up! But the bad bear stood at the bottom, growling as he said, 'I will get you!'"

He did a voice for each character and was much better at story time than I'd ever been. Case in point, Lennon only asked for him now when it was time to get in bed. She told me it was because, "Jake better at stories, Mommy," while she'd gently patted me on the arm. I'll admit I'd teared up then, partly because she wanted someone else besides me, but also because she seemed to be growing up in front of my eyes.

"Get away, you mongrel!" Jake made a swishing sword noise and pretended to be Prince Charming, fighting off the bear.

He looked to her for a reaction, but little miss was already yawning, her eyes closed and her hand twirling in a curl.

I stand in the doorway, watching as he puts a finger to his lips and scoots out of the bed as if he might just wake the sleeping dragon. I have to put my hand over my mouth to not let the laughter out as he crosses the room on his tiptoes as if the rug was made of hot lava. Together, we look back on her, sunken down into her pillows now, and turn off the light.

"I swear, every time I accomplish putting her to bed, I feel like I've run twenty-six point two miles. We will never in our life have to run a marathon, because we have a kid."

His use of the word *we* made butterflies swirl in my stomach. Why was the best thing in the world a goofy leftovers dinner in my apartment with my boyfriend and daughter? There was one time in my life where expensive shoes and traveling the world would have been my biggest goals. Now? I was sublimely happy with cold Chinese and a *Bloodline* binge on the couch.

"Wait for Christmas season. You'll feel like you did an Iron Man." I sat down on the couch, stretching my legs out and trying to fight off the Sunday Scaries. "Do we have to go back to work tomorrow?"

Jake sat beside me, taking my feet in his lap and massaging them. "Yes, we do. But maybe if you're lucky I'll swing by with a surprise at lunchtime."

Three times this month, Jake had swung by with lunch. I was beginning to get spoiled, and fat. I guess that wasn't to be helped if your boyfriend was a dessert chef and had connections at all of the best restaurants in town.

He set my feet down, and was fiddling with something in his pocket that he couldn't seem to get out.

"Do you really need to check your phone right now? Aren't the Nationals on rain delay?" I whine, mostly because the foot rub felt good and I didn't want him to stop.

He then got down on the floor, and I was even more annoyed thinking he dropped the damn device. He fumbled for a minute, and I laid my head back, reveling in the silence with Lennon asleep.

"Babe, can we just massage my legs more?" I kicked said legs out, whining more.

"I was going to wait until tomorrow at lunch to do this, with the truck all dressed up and ice cream spelling out the words or something. But this thing has been burning a hole in my pocket all night, and I don't want to wait another second."

I look back up, having no clue what this man is talking about, and my heart catches in my throat.

There, on the living room floor, kneels Jake. With a small box in his hand, opened up to reveal a sparkling diamond ring.

"Samantha, will you marry me?" His voice is so hopeful, his green eyes shining up at me.

"Are you fucking crazy?" The words pop out before I can control them.

He shakes his head, laughing. "I've been told at times I can be, but in all honesty, I've never been more sane than in this moment."

"It's crazy, Jake! We've only been dating for a few months!" My head spun as I looked at the ring.

He stayed on one knee, the sound of Lennon's ballerina music box tinkling in the background.

"Samantha, you waited years before. You told me you never thought you were enough, that there was something wrong with you because he wouldn't commit. Well here I am, telling you that I am so serious about you and I, and that little girl, that I want in forever. It doesn't matter if I've known you five years or five minutes, you are it for me. I want to make us a family, and I'm telling you that for me, you are always enough. More than enough. So marry me. Live your life with me. Live our lives together. Give that beautiful girl a bunch of brothers and sisters. We can get a dog if you want, or gerbils. Hell, I don't care. Just say yes."

I can taste the saltiness of my tears as I hiccup, love and overwhelming emotion swamping my heart and mind. We may have been together only a few short months, but he was right. This was so different than any relationship I'd ever been in. He was steady, caring, committed, loved Lennon. And I was in love with him, every quirky, annoying, workaholic part of him. Jake was the first person I wanted to tell about my day, he was the one I wanted to look at across the dinner table. I'd waited so long last time for validation, that it felt insane to get it so quickly now. But … when I'd moved here I had vowed to be open to whatever life had in store for us. And it turned out, love and Jake were it.

"Yes … yes, Jake, I will marry you," I whisper it, the words feeling too grand to be said fully.

He hops up off his knee, catching me in a hug and lifting me off my feet. The living room whirls in my vision, and I'm caught in a stir of emotions that I can't place words to. Everything inside of me feels overwhelmingly *happy* … it's akin to the first time I ever held Lennon in my arms.

Looking down my arm as Jake kisses my cheeks, I catch the flash of the ring.

And it is gorgeous. Not that that's the most important part of this moment, but a good ring is always something to be appreciated. It's a simple, thin silver band topped with an oval diamond surrounded by a halo of smaller diamonds. It glints even in the dim light of the living room, and my girly heart falls in love with it instantly. Even though I'd thought so much about getting engaged in the past, I'd truly never thought of what kind of ring I'd like.

"How did you pick it out? It's perfect, baby."

"You didn't think Lila was just in town to hang out with you, did you?" My eyes skim down to his lips, which are parted in a mischievous smile.

"Are you kidding me?! That little sneak." I couldn't believe it.

We'd had a great long weekend together, and in the background, she'd known that Jake was about to ask me to marry him the whole time. Shit, I had a great best friend.

"Thank you for not doing some big thing like flying me up in a hot air balloon."

"I was thinking of riding in on an elephant to your parking lot at work, but then thought better." That dimple pops out.

"This was perfect, just us. How it always should be." I look at the ring again, shocked at how beautiful it is, and that there is that significant piece of jewelry sitting on my left hand.

"Should we wake Lennon up?" His hands move up under my shirt, finding my bare skin.

I nuzzle into his neck. "That depends, did you want sex or not? Because you know that if we wake the sleeping beast, you'll have no alone time with me tonight."

"In that case, let me introduce you to my sleeping beast." He takes my left hand, the one with the large rock on the fourth finger, and puts it over his sweatpants where he is growing.

"My fiancé is so corny." I swish the word around in my mouth, testing it like every new engaged girl imagined she would.

"Say it again." Jake moves over me, my body molding to his as he leans me back into the couch.

"*Fiancé*," I whispered in my best phone sex voice.

"Oh yeah, baby ..." He smiles and shakes his head as if I'm turning him on so much by uttering the word. "Now come here and let me finish that proposal. Because I can make it so much sweeter."

EPILOGUE
JAKE

One Year Later

"I thought we said we'd talk about getting a different mattress." I shift my weight, groaning as I threw an arm over Samantha.

"Nope, this one is perfect. Pillowy softness." She grins as she melts into me, kissing my stubbly morning cheek.

"It's like laying on a bunch of pillows. A mattress should be firm, have a backbone like hardwood." I grunt, thrusting my hips against her, my cock pressing to her thigh.

"Honey, what's mine is yours, and marriage is all about compromise. Or at least, it will be starting today."

"It's wedding day!" Lennon ran into our room, launching herself at the bed and giggling as she snuggled herself between us. I scooted over, making sure to cover my nether regions with a pillow, even as I felt myself shrink. It was amazing what kids could do to the libido.

She ran her hands over Samantha's face, mussing up her hair in a way that she must have thought looked pretty, but really made my fiancée look like a witch.

"Are you ready for your flower girl duties?" Samantha kissed Lennon's cheek and wrestled her down, pinning her arms so she couldn't mess up her long dark locks any more.

"I have my basket all ready. I practiced last night with Dad."

My heart absolutely puddled at my feet. I wouldn't be surprised if it was lying in a mushy pool on the floor at the edge of the bed. For the last six months, ever since Lennon had really grasped that we were all officially going to become a family, she'd been calling me Dad. Never Daddy, that was the name she used for Derek, but I was so honored to hold that title in her life.

"You'll be so pretty." I kiss her forehead as she snuggles between Samantha and me.

Over the past year, we've become even more of a family than I even knew was possible. Growing up in a family like mine, we weren't necessarily close. Competition and business ruled the roost there, and they had ever since. But Samantha, Lennon and I ... we did everything together. They supported me on late nights when the restaurant was crazy, and I'd drop from exhaustion the minute I got home. I picked up Lennon from daycare and made dinner, carried the laundry downstairs to the basement of the building when we needed to do it. Family movie nights on Friday were a thing of tradition now, and Samantha and I typically had date night once a week. On weekend mornings, Lennon came to the restaurant with me and brought customers in. She was probably single-handedly responsible for half the business that walked inside the place; her cute little diatribes near the front door always drew people in.

We burned dinner together, and then ordered pizza. We went on walks around the city blocks that made our feet tired and ended up with Lennon sleeping on my shoulder. Apartment hunting for a place that was big enough for three of us was a trip, with Samantha's checklist and mine clashing so much that we ended up learning a lot about each other. Lennon begged us for a puppy every other week, and I think that my soon-to-be wife was starting to break. Each one of us fought for the last Magnum bar in the freezer ... Samantha always won. We celebrated birthdays, slept in on the weekends when we could, and for the first time last year I'd had a real Christmas tree. Samantha had insisted, it wasn't the holiday without one.

Our new place between my office building and Samantha's was a two bedroom, with an extra bathroom than either of us had had before, and a larger kitchen. It also boasted a patio, which we made full use of almost year round ... even when we had to throw gloves and coats on.

In our apartment, it was business as usual. I manned the scrambled eggs, Lennon helped with juice duty, and Samantha sat at the table reading The New York Times. We gave her weekend mornings off, calling our little breakfast act, "the toastsome twosome." If it weren't for the butterflies in my stomach, and the fluffy white dress hanging in the closet in our bedroom, you wouldn't know that we were about to say some vows and exchange some rings today.

After she's done eating, I look over to where Lennon is sitting on the living room floor, taking off her Barbie's pants again.

"Lennon, leave those on." What was with this little girl wanting her dolls to be nudists? "And yes, after the wedding I made you a special ice cream cake."

It was my first foray into cakes, and I'd insisted on making our wedding cake. I pat myself on the back, because this cake was fucking gorgeous. I was going to have Alice post pictures of it on the company Instagram and see what response we got. We could make some big bucks if I started doing cakes to order.

"I can have three pieces!" She claps.

"Oh yeah, who said that?" Samantha makes a sarcastic, shocked expression at me.

"I did. Grandma said so too."

"That Grandma spoils you, huh?" I finish my coffee and lace my fingers through Samantha's. "You ready to get married to me?"

"That depends ... do I get that foot rub I was promised?" She props her feet up on my lap, her toes a light pink.

Is it weird that even her feet are sexy to me? Because I swear, I'm sporting a semi.

"I think I'm like your foot rub slave for the rest of my life. Isn't that what marriage means?"

She nodded, her face pointed toward the ceiling as I rubbed her insoles. "Pretty much."

"Should we go become the Brady bunch?" It was time to get moving if we were going to make our own ceremony.

Samantha shudders. "Oh God, please don't start that again."

I start to hum the theme song to the popular TV show. I'd been joking about it since we'd gotten engaged, knowing that she hated when I called us that.

"I'm not walking down that aisle if you keep doing that." She leaned over, slapping her hand over my mouth.

Little did she know that I'd already made it our official wedding hashtag and told the short number on the guest list about it.

Oh well, she'd have to live with it. She'd have to live with me. That was marriage. Taking the annoying with the amazing. And I was definitely getting the best of both worlds.

Sometimes I thought to myself, how did I get so lucky? But really, I think I'd charmed or tricked them into picking me. I was fine with that, as long as it meant I got to come home to those two at the end of the day.

Damn, my priorities had changed. What had once been one-night stands and a good bottle of red became romance and sippy cups.

Bring on the minivan.

L ooking for another romantic comedy to make you crack up and warm your heart? Read <u>Save the Date</u>, a marriage pact romance!

ALSO BY CARRIE AARONS

Do you want your **FREE** Carrie Aarons eBook?

All you have to do is <u>**sign up for my newsletter**</u>, and you'll immediately receive your free book!

Then, check out all of my books, available in Kindle Unlimited!

ABOUT THE AUTHOR

Author of romance novels such as Fool Me Twice and Love at First Fight, Carrie Aarons writes books that are just as swoonworthy as they are sarcastic. A former journalist, she prefers the love stories of her imagination, and the athleisure dress code, much better.

When she isn't writing, Carrie is busy binging reality TV, having a love/hate relationship with cardio, and trying not to burn dinner. She lives in the suburbs of New Jersey with her husband, two children and ninety-pound rescue pup.

Please join her readers group, Carrie's Charmers, to get the latest on new books, exclusive excerpts and fun giveaways.

You can also find Carrie at these places:

Website
Amazon
Facebook
Instagram
TikTok
Goodreads

Printed in Great Britain
by Amazon